Bitter Water

Books by R.G. Yoho

Long Ride to Yesterday
Boot Hill Valley

Kellen Malone Series
Death Comes to Redhawk
Death Rides the Rail

Coming Soon!
Nightfall Over Nicodemus
The Evil Day
Palo Duro
Return to Matewan
America's History is His Story

**For more information
visit:** www.SpeakingVolumes.us

Bitter Water

R.G. Yoho

SPEAKING VOLUMES, LLC
NAPLES, FLORIDA
2023

Bitter Water

Copyright © 2023 by R.G. Yoho

All rights reserved. No part of this book may be reproduced or transmitted in any form or by any means without written permission.

ISBN 979-8-89022-014-1

I dedicate this book to my daughter, Kaity, and all the other strong, independent, loving, and resourceful women in my life.

"Water is the driving force of all nature."
—Leonardo da Vinci

Chapter One

The porcelain teacup of water went flying across the room, just missing Sarah Crenshaw's head, the teacup shattering against one of the photos on the wall. The wooden picture frame and the glass that enclosed the photograph were shattered into many smaller pieces. The water soaked the wall and dripped from the frames of the unbroken photos that hadn't been struck.

"You had no reason to do that, Ben," she said.

"The hell I didn't," he replied. "I asked for whiskey, not water. Ain't no reason for your continual yammering on me. You cain't make no teetotaler out of me, not like your dead old man."

Ben rummaged through all the drawers and cupboards, trying to find one of his stashed bottles of whiskey. He ripped a couple of drawers from their slots, leaving them on the floor, their contents scattered around where they fell. The once-tidy house now looked as if it had been ransacked by looters.

"Where's my liquor, woman?"

"I threw it out, Ben, all of it."

"You didn't?"

"Yes, I did. It's all gone." She gently touched his arm. "Please, let me make you some coffee."

Ben shook away the soft hand from his arm. "I don't want coffee. I don't want water. I want whiskey. Now tell me where my bottle is."

"I told you already. It's gone, Ben. I poured it down the sink."

Ben still refused to believe her, ripping open a couple of the cabinets, loosing one of the doors from off its hinges.

Then he remembered his one special hiding place, a spot still unknown to Sarah. He snatched a knife from the cabinet and pried loose a board near the mantel. Once it was free, he threw the knife back on the kitchen table. Ben clutched the half-full bottle like it was a precious child. He wiped the dust from the bottle on his shirt, removed the cork, and took a long pull of the whiskey.

In that moment, the drink was all that really mattered to him.

Sarah Crenshaw had never been a woman alone, but she felt alone now.

Against her father's wishes, she married a small, local rancher when she was only fourteen. Ben Crenshaw was fifteen years older than Sarah. When she walked home from the tiny, one-room schoolhouse, Ben often left his chores early to ride by and court her affections.

Like any impressionable young woman, Sarah was soon smitten by the rancher's attention. Love certainly isn't blind, but its poor vision is often the enemy of common sense. As she followed the road back to her house, Ben would ride alongside, exchanging pleasantries.

Her papa often warned her that Ben was not someone to be trusted, "Not a man of good devices," that was how her papa described him. The father made even more derogatory statements about the man to Sarah's mother, figuring that Ben's interest in their daughter was nothing more than carnal.

Sarah failed to see the flaws her papa instantly detected in the man. But her father's entreaties did not go completely unheeded. Over time, they began to have an impact on Sarah's way of thinking. Ben saw it too; he sensed that the young woman was becoming somewhat distant and less interested in spending time with him.

That all changed with the fire.

Tragically, a brutal fire swept through their ranch house one overcast, April morning while Sarah was in school. Her father and mother were later found amongst the charred remains. Nobody seemed to know the cause of the fire or why her father had been inside the house, instead of out tilling his fields. The only thing people knew for certain is that it had been a great and unfortunate tragedy, for both them and their young daughter.

Unsure of what she should do, uncertain of where she should go, Sarah turned towards the only person, other than her parents, who had ever shown any special warmth for her. She found solace in the arms of Ben Crenshaw.

They were married only a couple of weeks later.

Unfortunately, young Sarah had yet to learn that marriages built on anything other than mutual love are generally constructed on a shaky foundation. In this case, their union soon began to crumble not long after their honeymoon.

It was then that Sarah also saw the numerous character flaws in Ben that her father had promptly recognized. The beatings started, although Ben only beat her when he was drunk.

Of course, he was drunk nearly all the time.

The situation was altered when Sarah became pregnant with little Sam. Ben promised that he would give up drinking while she was carrying their child. And things did change for a while. Once again, Ben returned to acting like the man she fell in love with, the one who often rode by and spoke so kindly to her when she walked home from school. Despite her misgivings, Sarah prayed that they had finally turned a corner and the peace and happiness that she long desired was now finally going to be hers.

Perhaps her papa had been wrong about him. Sarah now felt real happiness, an apparent state of marital bliss which continued for over two full years after the birth of their child.

Yet when Sam was nearly three, Ben returned to the bottle.

Not long after Ben returned to drinking, Sarah discovered the gold watch, an item that always accompanied her father. He never left the house without that watch hanging in his vest pocket.

It had been hidden in the back, right corner of Ben's desk.

That evening, a puzzled Sarah asked her husband about it. He set down the whiskey bottle long enough to say that her father must have given it to him. Upon explaining that her papa treasured that watch as a gift from his grandfather and planned to give it to his own grandson someday, Ben changed his story, claiming that he found it on the ground outside her parents' home after the fire.

Only lately had Sarah begun to give some serious consideration to what her husband's possession of the watch might mean. Even more fearful was what it might mean in regards to the deaths of her father and mother.

But Sarah was not a fool.

She just tried not to think about it. Dwelling on the reasons why Ben had her father's watch was too painful for her. Increasingly, Ben's drinking and abuse made it more difficult to put those thoughts, fears, and conclusions in the back of her mind.

On this day, Sarah was once again reminded of her father's warnings.

For a time, she said nothing as she watched him drink. "You happy now, Ben? At least you've got the only thing you really want to keep you warm at night, whiskey."

A slap alongside her jaw sent Sarah reeling across the top of the table and spilling her onto the floor on the other side. She reached up to touch the painful spot on the side of her jaw. When she pulled her hand away, she was startled to see the sight of blood. Her own blood, flowing from a cut on the side of her mouth.

Her husband lifted a nearly empty liquor bottle to his lips.

"Why are you doing this, Ben?" Sarah said, still speaking from her place on the floor. "You told me you were done with the whiskey."

"A little drink now and then won't do me no harm."

"A little drink, you say? Looks like you've almost drank the whole bottle."

"Mind your own damn business, woman. I'll drink when I feel like it."

"But you said you would stop when the baby was born."

"I did stop."

"But now you're drinking again."

Ben tossed down the last of the liquor and tossed the bottle on the floor beside him. He wiped his mouth on the sleeve of his shirt, picked up his hat, started towards the door.

"Where are you going, Ben?"

"Just never you mind, woman. I have to ride into town and get me another bottle."

"Please, Ben," she said, throwing her harms around him. "Don't go. You've had enough liquor for tonight. Wouldn't you rather stay here with me and little Sam?"

Ben shrugged his shoulders and shook her off.

"Please don't go," Sarah said again.

At that moment, little Sam came in from the other room and walked towards the door. "Please don't go, Papa," the little boy said.

"See, woman, now you've got him doing it too." Having said that, the drunken husband struck his wife with his open hand, sending her much smaller body reeling across the room.

Still hurting from the blow and the fall, she looked up at her husband from the floor. "Why do you always have to hurt me? Papa was right about you, Ben. You aren't a man of good devices."

"Your papa, you say? That old bastard never did like me, Sarah. He got what he had coming. Never should have tried to stop me from seeing you," Ben said, the liquor freeing his tongue to reveal the deeper truths he'd always kept hidden.

"When I refused to listen to your old man, he gave me a good thrashing, the likes of which I hadn't seen since my own daddy done it to me years ago. He didn't give me no choice; I had to shoot him. When your ma came to his aid, I knew I had to keep her from talking to the sheriff. Afterward, I put their bodies inside the house and set it on fire. Don't try and pretend you didn't figure it out, Sarah. You already know about your old man's watch."

"I thought it might be true, but I wasn't sure until now. You monster! You didn't need to kill them."

Ben sprang upon his fallen wife like he planned to beat her again. He straddled the woman, like a hunter getting ready to gut a fallen buck. He raised his hand like he planned to strike Sarah again.

"Don't hurt mama," the child said, scurrying over to help his mother.

Ben slapped little Sam across the face, knocking aside the small child like someone tossing around a rag doll. Until this moment, Ben's drunken escapades only led him to curse or beat his wife, conditions for which Sarah often blamed herself or her behavior.

This, however, was different.

Now, Ben had slapped her son.

This time, his actions were more than she could stand.

Ben turned on his heel and staggered towards the door. The woman's pain was overwhelmed by her rage. Sarah leaped to her feet and said, "Nobody harms my child." She seized the knife from the table and plunged it clear to the hilt, deep into her drunken husband's back, before pulling it out.

Blood splashed from the wound, marking her dress and spilling onto the floor. With Ben's eyes wide and disbelieving, he turned to face Sarah, who was still holding the bloody knife. "Dammit, woman, you've kilt me," he said, raising his fist, as if to strike her again, before collapsing on the floor.

Throwing down the bloody blade, Sarah wasted no time. She snatched up her son, shielding his eyes from the carnage. Sarah carried him into the bedroom and threw some of their clothes into a satchel. After lifting a loose board of her own in the closet, she reached in and removed the few meager dollars of cash she managed to squirrel away from her drunken husband.

Sarah then rushed into the kitchen and shoved some biscuits and other provisions into her bag. She also grabbed some cooking utensils and other items as well. Thinking she had everything she needed, Sarah lifted Sam in her arms, taking one last look at this man she once loved, before going out the door.

On second thought, Sarah gently set him down on the porch. "You wait for me here, Sam," she said, going back inside the house. Stooping alongside her fallen husband's body, Sarah fished inside his vest pocket for the gold watch. Once in possession of her father's treasured keepsake, she kissed the watch and returned outside to join her son.

A small tear moistened Sarah's eye, but it changed nothing. It was one thing for Ben to get drunk and slap her around, but the woman was determined that nobody was ever going to lay an angry hand on her son.

Ben's horse was already saddled outside the house, so she lashed their belongings behind the saddle. She loosed the reins and led the tall horse alongside the steps, something that would make it easier for her to slip her foot into the horse's stirrups. Then she placed her son atop the saddle and swung herself onto the leather. Shaking out the reins, Sarah started down the trail, destination unknown.

All Sarah knew is that she wanted to get away.

The two of them rode for several hours when Sarah checked the canteen. Upon fleeing the house, she saw the canteen hanging from the saddle and assumed it was full. She almost cursed when she realized it was almost empty.

Sarah laughed without humor. It shouldn't have surprised her that the man who always had a full bottle of whiskey waiting to relieve his thirst also made no provisions for having plenty of water to drink.

Sarah lifted the canteen and did little more than barely wet her lips. She saved several big gulps for her thirsty son.

"That's all there is, Sam. Your mama is going to have to find a watering hole pretty soon or we're both going to be in big trouble."

Chapter Two

Four weary but determined men remained at the card table as the sun rose in the eastern sky. Their card game had continued through the night, nobody willing to walk away, a couple of the players suffering significant losses, the other two still not holding the final stakes they desired to have when they left the table.

Hoping to catch a few hours of sleep, the bartender had long since gone home for the night, leaving a couple of bottles and glasses for the players before he departed. Upon returning, getting ready for the morning breakfast crowd, he was surprised to see the men had not stopped their poker game.

"Any of you boys want coffee?" he said.

A couple of the players nodded. The barkeep started preparing a pot of coffee and then carried an empty tray over to their table. He removed several of their empty glasses, placing them on a tray, along with the empty bottles.

Jason Evers, a professional gambler, grabbed the bartender's hand to stop him when he tried to remove his glass or the near-empty whiskey bottle. "Thanks, mister," he said, with a smile, "but those stay."

Evers poured himself another glass of whiskey, drinking it down in a gulp.

The game continued, long after the bartender brought them their coffee and returned to top off their cups. In the meantime, Jason Evers had seen his stakes grow and one of the other players finally drop out of the game.

Evers was an excellent poker player, schooled in the intricacies of the game early, learning them from an uncle, who earned his living for many years as a riverboat gambler. The uncle only gave up the game when he nearly drowned upon the sinking of the steamboat, *Arabia*, on the Missouri River in 1856, but finally played out his hand at Chancellorsville in 1863.

Evers, who considered his uncle a hero, sought to follow in the man's footsteps, except for the bad parts about dying in the war or nearly drowning with the *Arabia's* lone mule on the wide Missouri.

Jason lost a couple of small hands, but routinely kept winning the bigger pots. Of the original four players who entered the game, only three remained. One of them, a small-time rancher, saw his stakes dwindle down to nothing, most of his money piled in front of Evers and the other gambler.

A closer look at his face revealed the small-time rancher's desperation and fear about his losses. The signs were obvious on his face. The rancher was an open book, an easy mark, displaying expressions that could easily be read by any professional gambler, qualities that made him unfit to match his skills against anyone seasoned in the game of poker.

Realizing the odds were not in his favor to win his money back, the rancher folded cards on his bad fortune and left the table, returning home to a long-suffering woman who would once again soundly chastise him for the precious money he squandered, along with his penchant for being out all night.

With only two players left in the game, Evers knew he was facing a man skilled in poker or the man's luck was certainly better than anyone he'd ever known. About twenty minutes later, Evers determined the man's winning couldn't be attributed to mere luck.

After watching him for a couple of more hands, the gambler knew the man was cheating. Normally, Evers would have forced the issue, but not on this day.

Jason had already earned more money than he brought to the table. Besides, there was a high-stakes poker game in another town that he soon planned to join. With that fact in mind, he wanted no trouble.

The other player raised after Jason's bet. Jason laughed without humor and merely folded. He started picking up his remaining winnings and began putting them in his pockets.

It was a substantial sum.

"What are you doing?" the other gambler said.

"I've had enough. I need to catch a couple hours of sleep." Jason stood up and began to push his chair back up against the table.

"You can't go now," the man said, grabbing his arm. "I was hoping to win a little bit more of those other fellows' money."

Evers looked down at the man's hand on his elbow and shook it off. "I suggest you just sit here at the table long enough and those other gents might be back. You can get it from them, but I'm done here."

The other gambler grew harsh. "You're done when I say you're done."

Evers just smiled at the belligerent gambler. "You might want to watch your tone with me, sir. I'm willing to let it go this time, figuring you might be a little tired too, after playing poker all night."

The other gambler jumped to his feet. "The only thing I'm tired of are your excuses for not playing another hand." About that time, he clawed for a gun, but already saw himself looking down the dark and deadly bore of Evers' pistol.

"I could kill you right here and now if I so desired, mister," Jason said. "And everybody in this room knows I could claim self-defense. But this is your lucky day, luckier than your numerable skills at the card table. I'm not going to kill you, but you've got two seconds to move your hand away from that gun."

As the other gambler contemplated his odds, he made no effort to move his hand away from the butt of his pistol.

"This isn't a game of cards," Evers added, "and I'm not bluffing."

After struggling to read Evers' face all night long at the poker table and learning nothing in his expressions, this time was different. He didn't know if Jason had the skills to beat him with a gun, but he also knew that Evers appeared confident enough in his abilities to call him out.

The other gambler swallowed hard and eased his hand away from the gun.

"That's much better," Jason said.

Jason Evers never holstered his gun. He did pause long enough to pour himself a final glass of whiskey with his left hand. He set down the now empty bottle on the table and picked up the glass with the same hand. Jason threw down the final gulp, smiled, and backed away from the table.

"Now I must bid you, sir, a most pleasant day."

Jason never showed his back again until he was safely out the door. Figuring he'd already more than worn out his welcome in that town, the few hours of sleep he longed to get would have to wait. Evers crossed the street to the hotel to get his belongings. Then he would return to the stable to retrieve his horse.

Another high-stakes poker game waited for Jason in the West; nothing but trouble waited for him here.

Evers knew the only winning hand was to fold his cards and ride away.

Chapter Three

The young boy stared down at the drought cracks in the soil and figured they were almost big enough to stick his hand into them without touching either side. Almost ready to test his theory, he stooped down and started reaching his hand forward until something more interesting caught his attention. The kid came to his feet and watched, using his hand to shield his eyes from the bitter rays of the sun.

The hooves of four distant horses and their riders kicked up a huge cloud of dust as they approached their ranch.

"Pa, some men are coming this way," Jimmy said.

"Yeah, I see them," Anse Willard replied, as he removed an already dampened rag from his back pocket to wipe away the salty sweat which was burning his eyes as it dripped into them.

It was much too hot a day to be splitting firewood, but Willard knew that winter's cold would find its way to them as certainly as the unbearable summer heat. Then, he would need every stick to keep the house warm and to prepare their daily eats.

"You think I should go and tell Ma, in case she wants to make them some grub?"

"Naw, Jimmy. Give her a few moments alone. She wanted to get a bath," he said, placing another log upright before splitting it down the middle with his maul.

"Now, you hurry back to the barn and finish watering the stock."

Jimmy just stood there, staring off into the distance, watching the men and horses come closer. The boy never got to town much. Like most children, he was fascinated by the lives and activities of those outside their small home and ranch. He wanted to remain with his father, to hear the men talk about other things and places unknown to him.

"Off with you now," Willard said. "I mean it. Get back out there and finish those chores."

"Yes sir," said Jimmy, slowly shuffling off to the barn.

Four hot, tired, and weary riders rode up to the ranch house as Willard continued splitting firewood next to the house. Their clothes were covered with road dirt, but their sweaty faces all shared a friendly smile upon seeing the young rancher.

"Good afternoon to you, Gents. My name's Anse, Anse Willard."

"Same to you, Mr. Willard," Hank Metcalf said, gently tipping his hat. "Pleased to make your acquaintance. These here are my friends and riding partners, Lefty, Bill, and Sid."

"Pleased to meet you. You're welcome to fill your canteens and water your horses from my well over there." He smiled. "It's good, sweet water."

"Thank you kindly, mister. It sounds inviting," Bill Ford said, stepping down from his horse, leaving the animal ground hitched. Then he picked up an extra maul and started to split firewood alongside the ranch owner.

"You don't have to do that, Mister."

"It's the least he can do to return your kindness," Metcalf said, climbing down from his horse. He handed the reins to Sid and Lefty, who took their tired and thirsty mounts over to the well.

He reached out and shook the rancher's hand. "You raise horses?"

"Yes, I do."

"You have any to sell?"

"Maybe half a dozen or so. They're all fine stock and are certain to earn high dollar."

"That's good to hear. It always makes me smile to see good people prospering. Nice place you have here."

"I think so. Me and the missus worked mighty hard to build it. Now little Jimmy does his share as well."

"Is he your boy?"

"Yeah, he's in the barn, watering the horses."

"Good thing to have," Hank said. "Obedient boy like that."

"I'm right proud of him."

"You should be," Hank said, lifting the dipper of water to his mouth from the bucket that Sid brought to him, after first serving a drink to Ford. Metcalf took another drink and then dropped the dipper back in the oaken bucket. Sid returned to the well and the horses. "That water's mighty tasty, sweet and cool. Me and the boys, here, are cowhands. You don't know anyone needing to hire some hands, do you?"

While Hank and Anse talked, Ford continued with the job of splitting firewood, leaving Anse pleased to see the work getting done while he enjoyed a small break. Lefty and Sid busied themselves with making sure their canteens were filled and the horses were watered.

"Can't say I do. But if you boys are hungry, I can have Sylvie make you something to fill your empty bellies. You'll have to wait until she finishes her bath first."

"She's taking a bath, you say?" Ford said, splitting another log right down the middle. He lifted his elbow to wipe a grubby shirtsleeve across his brow. "That sounds right refreshing. I ain't had one of them in a couple of weeks. You know, Hank, we're going to have to get one of them when we get into town."

"That's not a bad idea, Bill. I'll keep it in mind."

It was then that Bill Ford stopped splitting wood and simply stood there with the maul resting on his shoulder. His mind on something else. Bill's eyes lifted from the woodpile, directing his gaze toward the windows of the ranch house.

"Is there any chance my friend Lefty could take a gander at them horses? We might be in the market real soon."

"Sure thing, Mr. Metcalf. Jimmy will show your friend the stock. He knows almost as much about them as I do."

"That's good," Hank replied, smiling.

Lefty started walking towards the barn.

As easily as the smile came to Hank Metcalf's face, it left him just as fast.

"Bill," Hank said, "maybe you should go and see if Sylvie's done with her bath. Her bath water might be getting cold."

"Sure thing," Bill said. "She might even need some help scrubbing her back."

Upon hearing those words, Anse's face was overtaken by a combination of fear and anger. He sprang towards his shotgun, which rested against a log yet to be split. Just as he caught up the weapon, a loop settled around his shoulders.

Sid Russell roped the man from horseback, threw a turn around the saddle horn, and started backing up his horse. Like the way a ranch hand would pull a steer towards the branding fire, Anse Willard was jerked from his feet and the shotgun discharged when he fell.

Meanwhile, Ford strolled towards the house, while Russell kicked his horse into a gallop, dragging the pained and screaming rancher out of the ranch yard.

At the sound of the shooting and yelling, Jimmy rushed out of the barn, only to be met by Lefty Pitts, armed with a knife. The boy barely made a sound before his voice was permanently silenced.

Inside the house, Sylvia Willard heard the gunshot outside. She scrambled out of the tub, wrapped herself in a couple of towels, and hurried down the stairs to see what was behind all the commotion. Water dripped from the woman's hair and unclothed body as she dashed down the stairs for the door.

"Anse," she shouted, "what's going on out there?"

As Sylvia placed her hand on the knob, the door opened from the outside.

"What's wrong, Anse?"

The door fully opened and Willard saw it was not her husband who entered the room. She was startled to be confronted by a stranger, a big silhouette that loomed inside the brightness of the open doorway.

Sylvia pulled the towel around herself tighter, her mind gripped with fear and bewilderment. "Where is Anse? Who are you? And what have you done with Jimmy?"

"I'm Bill Ford. Your husband won't be joining us, Sylvie. Neither will your son. They're both resting now. And you and me should have plenty of time to get to know each other a mite better."

Tears filled the frightened woman's face as she wheeled around to race for the stairs, but not before Ford snatched at her towel and pulled it from her body. She sprinted up the stairs to get away from the stranger. Ford simply kicked the door closed behind him and calmly ambled up the staircase.

Chapter Four

The first brilliant rays of dawn were just breaking over the distant horizon, starting to overpower the flickering lights of the nearby town as a single Indian rode back towards his camp. His heavily muscled body, bronze and bare from the waist up, sat upon the spotted, Indian pony. He rode bareback, almost like someone who had become one with the animal's every movement.

Already this morning, the sun was blistering the ground, with deep, dry cracks in the earth, places where the voices of the parched earth cried out for rain, dew, or just about any kind of moisture to relieve its suffering. There hadn't been a drop of water in over two weeks. That fact made no difference whatsoever to the rider.

He could go for days on little or no water.

Unsatisfied with his status in the tribe, the young warrior was always on a mission to impress the older, more experienced braves with his courage. He never missed a raiding party with the others, but this time he rode alone.

Kicking Deer was a young warrior with something to prove.

He spent little time worrying about the thoughts of the older braves, those who considered his actions reckless and unwise. In his mind, only fools and cowards concerned themselves with prolonging their departure into the next life. Kicking Deer was not afraid of death. He believed that those who are truly brave should welcome its arrival. Moreover, he could see nothing to be feared by joining the vast hunting parties of his ancient forebears in the next life.

He also believed that any warrior was invincible when the Great Spirit chose to ride with him. Kicking Deer had also seen how the guns of his white enemies fell silent or were rendered useless in earlier battles when employed against him. Many had been the time they fired their weapons at him, only to miss. He also knew that he had slain most of those men who unsuccessfully tried to kill him.

Those victories had greatly built his confidence.

It was obvious that the Great Spirit had already blessed his fortunes, a fact manifested by the seven white men's scalps that he had lifted. His blade had often tasted of the white men's blood and thirsted for more.

Kicking Deer also possessed nine excellent horses, in addition to the fleet, young steed he was now riding. Those animals were stolen from the ranches of the Whites or taken from his enemies, several of which he had killed and scalped, trophies of war that now hung from his belt.

Along with his desire to be considered a brave who possessed "big medicine" among his people, Kicking Deer was also a young brave in love with a beautiful young maiden of only fourteen winters. But his weren't the only eyes that wanted and longed to win the hand and affections of Blue Dove. This fair Indian maiden had no less than a dozen willing suitors among those in his camp.

Her father told Kicking Deer and the others that they must first deliver ten horses to him, in order to purchase the right to marry his youngest daughter. Kicking Deer thought the maiden would still be a bargain for twice that many horses.

A number of the other braves had acquired six or seven mounts, still several short of what her father required. Although he still only needed to steal one more before he could make Blue Dove his own, Kicking Deer still feared that the other braves might have a prosperous raid, gaining enough horses to take the woman he wanted.

This was another battle that Kicking Deer had no intention of losing. He was determined to make Blue Dove his own and to bring the young Indian maiden into his own lodge.

Kicking Deer had been out all night, but enjoyed no success on his plans to raid the stock pens of the Whites. On this night, he learned that their camps either had their horses secured inside their strong, wooden barns or their mounts tied up with trace chains, which could not be cut loose with his blade.

It was indeed a rare time when the spirits did not choose to shine on Kicking Deer. His successes had been many. As the weary young discouraged brave returned to his camp, he happened to cross the trail of a single, shod horse. His dark eyes twinkled at the sign. This was just the opportunity he'd been seeking.

He raised his eyes in thanks to the Great Spirit.

This was not the track of an animal he recognized. Climbing off his horse to check the sign, Kicking Deer saw it was a horse that had obviously just come from town. The sign was fresh, indicating that he was not far behind the rider.

The Indian knew he would have no difficulty catching up to the lone rider. Still, he knew nothing of the one who was mounted upon the horse. Perhaps the horse rider was a strong warrior. Kicking Deer would welcome that possibility, for it would give him another chance to test his own strength in battle.

He climbed back on his horse and started following the tracks. He only needed one more horse to win the hand of Blue Dove. Perhaps he would also take another scalp for his belt.

The spirits had indeed smiled down on him today.

Chapter Five

The lone rider drew rein at the top of the hill. Sitting there astride his horse, leaning both elbows on the saddle horn, he cast his gaze out over the rows of stones. Even though dozens of them had been erected there, each individual marker was imbued with a certain, distinct loneliness.

Two of them in particular held a special sadness for the rider.

For over twenty-four months, unless he was in pursuit of an outlaw, the marshal made this daily trek early in the morning, before he ever tasted his first sip of coffee.

He even took up drinking for a time and discovered that it actually helped him to forget, mainly in the hours while he remained good and drunk. But the man also learned that the biggest problem with using liquor as a tonic occurred when one needed to get sober. Perpetual drunkenness simply wasn't worth the other problems it caused. The drinking also put his job at risk . . .

It also jeopardized the marshal's reputation, something his late wife valued much more than he did.

For the sake of his wife's memory, the marshal set aside the bottle, except for an occasional nip, which he believed never did a man any lasting harm.

He climbed down from his horse, dropped the reins, and ventured inside the small iron gate. Walking respectfully through the midst of the cemetery, staying in the rows, careful not to step on any of the gravesites, United States Marshal Braxton Poole saw none of the names except for the specific two which shared his own last name.

The path he followed through the markers never varied. In fact, the marshal's daily visits were enough to ensure that the grass no longer grew where he walked, even in those times when rainfall was normal and abundant.

Upon seeing the pair of names, the marshal removed his hat.

Katherine Beatrice Poole, Beloved Wife and Mother.
Adam Braxton Poole, Beloved Son.

Poole stood there in silence, the seconds and minutes passing, until the man had not moved in more than an hour.

As his eyes once more drifted over the names, the grief Poole felt was almost as palpable as the final, tragic seconds when Katherine passed away, only moments after giving birth to Adam.

Today marked the two-year anniversary.

As if his wife's loss wasn't already pain enough for one man to bear, the doctor could do nothing to save the child either. Even the doctor couldn't explain why the child died as well.

The marshal remembered their deaths like it was only yesterday. But his eyes held no hint of a tear. Those dried up a long time ago, like the current, brutal drought that brought leanness to the fields and hardship to those brave and hardy souls who struggled to raise up crops from the unyielding dust.

For two long years, holidays had come and gone unnoticed, once-precious celebrations which used to hold great value to Braxton Poole and his wife. Instead, those festive occasions were often just stark reminders of the life and loves which the marshal no longer enjoyed.

He cursed them all.

"Good morning, Katherine. Howdy, Adam. How are you both doing today?"

Immediately upon the words leaving his mouth, Poole knew his remarks sounded stupid. The two of them were dead. The dead could rest in peace, but there could never be any lasting rest for those who survived them.

Poole hadn't experienced a truly restful night in two years.

He struggled with somehow voicing the sentiments that were now in his heart, things he needed to say, painful words he mostly needed to hear himself say.

"I've been coming here almost every day for two years and I fear it's done none of us any lasting good. It's clear I'm not going to get either of you back. Apparently, the Lord thought he needed you there more than I needed you here. Blessed be the name of the Lord, although I don't think it's in my heart to ever fully forgive him.

"This is going to be the last day I come here, Katherine. No, I'm not saying I won't return from time to time, to see that your resting place is adequately cared for, but I won't be here on a daily basis.

"You have little Adam to look after you now, and the Lord to care for both of you. If I'm condemned to walk this world without you, I reckon it's about time I got started on making it happen."

Marshal Poole stood there silent for a few moments, still searching for more words to express the thoughts on his mind and heart.

"I love you, Dear. I'll always love you. I've just recently come to realize that the way things are, ain't neither one of us doing much living. I trust you'll take care of little Adam for me. It's probably better that he wound up with you anyway. Not sure I would have been much of a father to him, at least not without your gentle hand to keep me somewhat civilized.

"Well, Dear, that's what I wanted to say. I hope you don't think I'm running out on you. That ain't what this is. So," he said, putting on his hat, "I'll be on my way now. I trust you won't forget me, neither."

Upon saying those final words, Marshal Poole didn't linger in front of the pair of cold, stone markers. He followed his usual, grassless path to the gate, went outside, and gently closed the gate behind him.

"Goodbye, Katherine," he softly muttered under his breath. "I'll never forget you."

Poole caught up his reins, forked his saddle, and reined his horse around to return to town. It was then he saw the horse and rider, a man just sitting off in the distance.

Poole was somewhat disappointed in himself, that he had failed to notice the man when he rode up. Finally, the marshal just chalked it up to the fact that he was so enthralled in his attention to the grave, he simply failed to notice.

Perhaps Poole was also human, a fact way too often pointed out to him by the man on the horse.

Poole knew the rider at a glance. It was Miles Olsen, a trusted friend and the town marshal about fifty miles from here. He also took note that the marshal was leading a pack horse. He knew that pack horse could only mean one thing, that Miles was hunting someone and needed some help.

He always knew Miles to be a tough and capable lawman, someone who generally handled his own affairs. The man was fair with a gun, and arguably, the best tracker that Poole had ever seen, who wasn't an Apache. If Miles was seeking his help, it must be something serious.

Upon seeing Poole moving in his direction, Marshal Olsen urged along his horses to meet him.

Chapter Six

Returning to consciousness, Ben Crenshaw lifted his head, while still lying on the ranch house floor. He cursed the pain he felt and the miserable, ungrateful woman who inflicted the serious wound upon him.

Ben reached around to his gaping wound and found it was still bleeding. Reaching up to the table, his searching hand found a dish towel and held it against the wound to stem the blood flow.

The loss of blood left him thirsty and lusting for a drink of water. Using the rails on the back of the chair for support, Crenshaw pulled himself to his feet. Since he was up and the bottle was still there, Ben took another drink of whiskey.

The liquor made him feel better about the pain, but it did absolutely nothing to relieve his gnawing thirst.

The wounded rancher was dizzy and uncertain on his feet. Bracing himself on the chair, he slid it alongside him to offer support as he walked. Slowly making his way over to the sink, Ben grabbed a now-cold, half-finished cup of coffee from off the counter. He dumped the remaining contents down the sink.

Unable to work the pump and catch a drink with only one hand, Ben was forced to let go of the dish towel, which caused his wound to resume bleeding. Once more he cursed his wife and vowed to find the wretched woman and kill her, just as soon as he recovered from his wounds.

Working the handle of the pitcher pump caused nothing but more pain for him, but Ben knew a bleeding man needed water. He finally pumped himself a cupful of water. He drank that one, followed by another.

It was then he heard a horse riding up to the house.

"It's that damned woman. Probably come back to finish the job, or to beg for my forgiveness. This time," he muttered, "I'm going to kill the whore."

While steadying himself against the counter, he drew his revolver from the holster and trained it on the door . . .

A door that was now opening.

* * *

As Jason Evers rode out of town, he was thinking about nothing other than the high-stakes poker game that waited for him west of here. The money he made in this last poker game was more than sufficient to meet the required entrance fee. He smiled at the fortune the game might offer him.

Due to the way he was leaving town, Jason didn't have a lot of time to make preparations. His canteen was low and his horse needed water. Both of those were bad situations to be in, considering the blistering heat which he faced.

About forty minutes out of town, the young gambler spotted a ranch house out in the distance.

Evers thought it might be a good place to water his horse and fill his canteen. As he drew closer, he could see this ranch was once a fine place, but the owner had obviously let it fall into disrepair lately. Some boards on the fences needed fixing. The barn door had dropped loose from one of its hinges. To the casual observer, there wasn't anything big, just minor chores left undone, items which would only grow more serious and damaging with continued neglect.

Drawing rein in front of the house, he tethered the horse to a dilapidated hitching rail. Then Jason started up the steps, pausing when he saw a bloody set of footprints headed in the opposite direction. He also detected a bloody handprint on the door jamb. In addition to all these things, the door also wasn't fully closed.

Uncertain of what happened in this house, or the unholy happenings which might even be transpiring inside at that very moment, Evers drew his gun and gently began pushing the door open with his left hand.

Before Jason could fully see what was on the other side of the door, a single gunshot sent a deadly slug only inches from where another quick step would have placed his body.

At the sound of the shot, Evers kicked the door fully open and triggered a fatal round into the blood-covered man standing in front of the sink. Jason's assailant never spoke, before crumbling to the floor in a heap.

Rushing over to the fallen rancher, Jason could see the man was already dead. It was also apparent that he had already been given a bloody head-start towards the afterlife, long before the young gambler arrived.

On the floor was a bloody knife, with a blade which clearly looked about the same size as the wound in the dead man's back.

"Looks like you went and angered the wrong person," Jason said, inspecting the room to understand what happened. "Bet you don't make that mistake again."

Evers found a small child's toys and clothing in one of the rooms, leading Jason to believe the child's mother and the rancher must have engaged in some sort of a heated argument. At some point, the gambler figured the dispute escalated to violence. It was then that the woman stabbed her husband in anger or in fear—perhaps both—running away and taking their child with her as she fled.

Jason speculated that she believed her husband was already dead when the woman left, but she was wrong. Despite the severity of the knife wound to his back, the rancher gamely survived. The young gambler, looking at the situation in the same manner he would evaluate the odds in a card game, wondered about the probabilities of any of this ever happening.

He couldn't help but laugh.

"Talk about a run of bad luck," Jason muttered. "Good thing you weren't a poker player, my dead friend." He paused to laugh at the odds of the situation's outcome. "You survived a potentially mortal knife wound, only to later be killed by someone who had the misfortune to happen upon this house, a mere stranger looking for water."

A stranger?

It was then that Jason realized the danger he faced. What if a friend or family member showed up here now?

It was certain he would be hanged.

Jason *was* a stranger here, an intruder at the scene of a man dead from knife and gun wounds. The dead man's gun also carried one spent cartridge, making it appear he was stabbed and simply attempted to defend himself.

If the young gambler was discovered in this situation, he doubted that anyone would believe an outsider's explanation in court. The local jurors obviously wouldn't be in his favor, leading Evers to wonder how he would avoid a guilty verdict.

And there was no doubt that the judge would sentence the young gambler to the gallows.

Jason swallowed hard and realized he needed to put some fast miles between himself and this cursed ranch house. Taking a few brief moments to wash the blood from his hands with water from the pitcher pump, the gambler stepped around the dinner table carnage and hustled back outside for his horse.

Leading the animal over to the well, he pulled up a bucket of water and filled his canteen. All he could think about was quickly getting away from here. Although Evers had never been a superstitious soul, he sensed that a dark, foreboding sense of danger still lurked around this ranch. Then Jason pulled up one more bucket and placed it in front of his horse. The animal buried its snout in the water and began to drink fully.

All at once, the buckskin mare quit drinking, lifted its head with a start, and nickered softly.

"What's the matter, girl? Is this place getting to you too?"

The words had no more than left the gambler's mouth before the ground darkened in front him with a shadow. Jason clawed for his gun, but it was too late. At that same moment, a bronze, heavily muscled arm choked off any chance for him to scream. From behind him, another bronze arm produced the glint of a blade.

He collapsed into the dust, blood and frothy bubbles coming from his throat, creating a crimson, muddy pool beneath him. As Jason Evers lay there dying, his dimming eyes watched the knife that just killed him slice away the cinch from his saddle, something for which the Indian had no need. The leather fell into the dust.

The Indian now had his horse.

Jason ceased to move.

His unseeing eyes failed to see the smile on the lips of Kicking Deer.

Chapter Seven

Kicking Deer leaned over the man's dead body and expertly lifted the gambler's scalp. He held his trophy high in the air, praising the spirits for once more making him successful on his solo raiding mission.

His was a daring kill and Kicking Deer was proud his victory was unaided by the darkness of nightfall. He also learned, to some dissatisfaction, that his White victim was clearly no great warrior among his people, for he offered the Indian brave no challenge whatsoever.

This victory over his enemy held no real glory.

After killing and scalping the gambler, he tied the man's horse to his own. Next, he crept up to the house and peered into the still open doorway. The Indian could see the blood all around the room. Kicking Deer marveled at the violence the Whites visited upon one another.

He went inside, grabbed the dead man by the hair, and lifted the man's head until Kicking Deer could see his face. He saw the dead man was the one they called 'Crenshaw.' After learning the identity of the dead one, the Indian dropped the man's head and it bounced off the floor once before lying still.

Kicking Deer guessed that Crenshaw's woman became angry and stabbed the rancher for the beatings and treating her in ways that he would never visit upon his love, Blue Dove. The Indian figured Crenshaw's bullet wound must have come from the scalped White, left dead and bleeding outside by the well.

For a couple of years now, Kicking Deer had longed to kill the rancher and steal his fine horse. Now the man was dead, killed by one of his own kind and his horse was missing from the open barn.

The Indian left the house, making no effort to take Crenshaw's scalp, because he placed no value on acquiring trophies from the kills made by others. Kicking Deer felt no remorse for Crenshaw's death, for the rancher had recently killed two hardy braves from his own tribe. His only regret was that his own blade had not been the one which took Crenshaw's life.

Kicking Deer knew it had been a good day. The Indian now had all the horses he needed to purchase his love from her father. As he started the return trip to his lodge, leading the dead gambler's horse, he came across the tracks of another mount.

Kicking Deer immediately recognized the tracks of this animal. It was the fine, powerful horse that belonged to Crenshaw.

He had once hidden out in the distant trees and watched the man, yelling at the young woman and beating her. Although the Indian was certain some women needed to be commanded with a firm hand, Kicking Deer knew this was not the way he would ever treat his dear, Blue Dove.

Throwing his leg up over his mount, he quickly dismounted, squatting down to study for signs. From the depth of the hoof falls, he guessed that this was a single rider, but it was a small man, unlike Crenshaw. Leading his mount, he walked along the tracks, giving them more careful study.

As he followed the trail on foot, the signs taught him even more about the rider. This was not someone making any effort to conceal his tracks. The rider was also not trying to save his mount. The horse moved like the rider was fleeing from something or someone.

He guessed it to be Crenshaw's woman, the one who stabbed him. The Indian smiled at the realization that she may have been a more formidable warrior than the one whose scalp he claimed back at the well.

It was then Kicking Deer found the remains of a cold biscuit, dropped upon the ground. He picked up the biscuit and could smell a woman's recent touch upon it. He carefully pondered what that information might mean. The rider had to be Crenshaw's woman; he was sure of it.

As Kicking Deer once more forked his horse, he smiled at his good fortune. But this situation also left him with a tough decision to make. The sun had climbed high into the sky. In addition, the Indian already had the horses he needed to purchase Blue Dove's hand.

Almost as much as he longed to have the respect of his elders and that of the other warriors in the tribe, Kicking Deer also desired to have the young maiden share his lodge and give him many strong sons.

But should he risk losing Blue Dove to another brave, in case one of them also enjoyed a successful raid and stole enough horses to win her hand? Or should he seek to enlarge his status among the tribe, by following this fine horse, killing the woman, and stealing her mount?

Kicking Deer had learned that the white men were weak, like children, and needed to drink water more often than his own people. He believed this knowledge gave him a distinct advantage over his enemies. If one knew where the water could be found, then one also knew the place where the Whites must eventually go.

A warrior had only to get to that location first and wait for them there. Once more, the Great Spirit had chosen to bless his efforts. He knew Crenshaw's strong horse would soon be his.

And the woman?

It was likely she would offer him little resistance before his blade once more tasted blood from the Whites.

Kicking Deer knew this would be much too easy. He only needed one more horse to claim his prize and he already took that one from the gambler. Perhaps it would be wise to take this opportunity to add another horse to his number. He knew that a strong warrior became mightier with the aid of a strong horse.

The precious, life-giving water this woman desired would soon become bitter to her taste. Forking his mount, Kicking Deer knew he must arrive at the nearest supply of drinking water before the woman did.

That knowledge was also tempered with the memory of his dead father's advice, to not anger the Great Spirit by being overconfident in one's ability to prevail over his enemies.

His dark eyes twinkled at the memory of his father's words, also at the realization that this small, White woman had somehow been able to plunge a blade into her much larger husband. The Indian thought it might be wise to remember this fact when he captured her.

The strong should not die from the hands of the weak.

His decision was made.

Kicking Deer would find Crenshaw's woman, kill her, and steal her horse. Then he would return to his tribe and claim his prize. The Indian cast one more thankful look towards the heavens and then started his horse down another path, riding towards the nearest place of water.

Perhaps Blue Dove would share his blanket very soon.

Chapter Eight

Upon riding up to meet the town marshal, Poole reached out to him, shook his hand and said, "Good morning, Miles."

"Same to you, Braxton," he replied, returning the handshake. He paused and looked out over the cemetery. "Still early in the morning and it's hotter than the red side of Perdition, ain't it?"

Still not in much of a mood for needless small talk, Poole smiled politely. "Hadn't really noticed."

"I figured you'd probably be here. It's been two years ago today, hasn't it?"

Poole merely nodded. "How long you been waiting for me?"

"Long enough."

"You could have let me know you were here."

"No, Braxton. No, I couldn't. A man shouldn't be interrupted while talking to those precious souls who have passed on. I tried to stay back out of earshot, because a man shouldn't be spied on at times like this either."

Poole nodded again. "I appreciate that. This is a bit far for an early morning ride, isn't it, Miles?" Then Poole cast a glance over towards the pack horse. "What can I help you with?"

"You know me too well."

"A lawman leading a pack horse visits the U.S. Marshal, thirty miles from his jurisdiction, it doesn't require much in the way of detective skills to figure that one out," Poole said. "Now tell me. What's the problem and who are we going after?"

Olsen lowered his head for a moment before speaking. When his head lifted again, there was the unmistakable glint of a tear in his eyes. "It's a bad one, Braxton. Maybe the worst I ever saw. Figured I needed some capable help. Besides, as you already said, they're out of my jurisdiction."

"But not mine?"

"Nope, but none of that really matters to me right now. I would follow this gang to hell if I had to, just to make them pay for what they've done. I'm guessing you ain't had your morning coffee yet, either."

"So, you know about that too, do you, Miles?" Poole said, with a knowing look in his eyes. "Not much escapes you."

"I *am* a town marshal, Marshal Poole. And I'm also your friend. You're not the only one who notices things. I'll buy you a cup of coffee before we leave."

"You can tell me about it on the way into town," Poole said. "I'll be needing to get just a few things, if I'm going to go with you."

"You won't need much, Braxton. Just make damn sure you bring that trusty rifle of yours. And get plenty of cartridges. I've got enough water, coffee, and supplies for the trip. I stocked enough for both of us."

"Sort of taking for granted that I'd go with you, wasn't you, Miles?"

"I had a hunch."

The two men started walking their horses down off the hill, the trail from the cemetery leading into town.

"Tell me about it, Miles."

"It's Hank Metcalf."

"Metcalf? Hoping he was dead by now."

"Lot of us hoping for that. You should have killed him, Poole, back when you had the chance."

"I got him thrown into prison."

"Lot of good it did. He's out again. It's a damned legal system we have nowadays, letting criminals go free without even paying for their crimes."

"You won't get any argument from me, Miles."

Marshal Olsen was silent for a few moments, as a man will often do in the moments just before he must offer up the accounts of an incident that he finds too distasteful to revisit.

"Do you remember Anse Willard?"

"Yeah, I do. Had a nice little spread next to the river, not too far from you," Poole said. "If I recall correctly, Anse had a wife. Sylvia was the name, I think. Fine woman. They were raising a stable of good horses. They had them a little boy too."

"Jimmy."

"Yeah, that was it. How are they doing?"

"They're all dead. Murdered."

"Dead? All of them?" Poole was shocked to learn about the murder of this fine, young family, all of them benevolent souls, folks who posed no threat to anyone.

"Yep."

This time it was Marshal Poole who dropped his head, shaken by the tragic loss of a kind and generous family.

"Hank Metcalf and his boys robbed a bank just to the southeast of here. He's running with three outlaws, Sid Russell and some younger kid, named Lefty Pitts. A posse tried to follow them, but Hank and his boys killed two from the posse and put the rest of them to flight with their long guns."

"Yeah, I've heard of Russell. Bad hombre. But the kid's name is unfamiliar to me. Wait a minute, Miles." Poole said. "You said there were three."

"I saved the worst name for last, Braxton," Olsen said, wiping the beads of sweat from his forehead on the elbow of his coat sleeve. "Hank's also running with Bill Ford."

"Bill Ford, the rapist? Now, there's a man I'd like to kill, with or without a warrant, if I ever placed my gun sights on him. And I wouldn't lose a minute's sleep over the doing of it too," Poole said. "But what's Metcalf and Ford have to do with the Willard family? Please don't tell me they . . ."

Olsen never let Poole finish the sentence. "It's true, Braxton. It was a scene worse than you can ever imagine. As best as we could tell, Metcalf's boys were needing fresh horses and happened upon the Willards' ranch."

Olsen stopped, clearing his throat before he regained composure.

"Take your time, Miles."

"Anse was dragged for about half a mile behind a horse," the marshal explained. "Predators got most of what was left of him. The little boy, Jimmy, he was knifed and left dead and bloody in the barn."

"What about the woman, Mrs. Willard?"

Olsen paused for several moments before he continued. His eyes filled with tears, not over her death, but over knowing the unspeakable brutality Sylvia Willard must have faced there in the long hours before she passed.

"We found Mrs. Willard in her bed, naked as the day she was born. I'm certain Bill Ford must have seen to her. Him and maybe some of the others. There wasn't a single drop of blood on her, except down there . . . you know."

Poole winced and nodded his head. "Yeah, I know."

"Except for some bruises, there really wasn't anything to explain why she died. I guess the loss and the repeated violations were too much for that good woman to bear. After they finished their unspeakable acts, Metcalf and his gang ransacked the house and swapped out their horses for fresh mounts," Olsen said. "I started tracking them, but there's too many for one man. And you're the best hand I know with a long gun."

The two men drew rein in front of Poole's house.

"Give me just a few minutes to gather my gear and I'll meet you at the diner. Along with the coffee, order me something to eat too. Once we finish, we'll get right back on their trail."

Braxton Poole swung down from his saddle and lashed his reins around the hitching rail.

"Thank you for agreeing to go with me, Braxton. The sight of that young boy's body and the condition of his mother will haunt me forever." Olsen once more wiped away the sweat on his forehead with his sleeve. He also wiped the moisture away from his eyes, something that wasn't sweat. "I was going after them anyway, but one man isn't capable of getting them all. And, besides . . ."

"Stop," Poole said, lifting his hand to stop his friend's further explanations. "It's my job, Miles. And in this case, it will be my distinct pleasure to help send Bill Ford off to meet the devil."

Chapter Nine

While still riding back to pick up the trail of the Metcalf gang, Marshals Poole and Olsen passed within eyeshot of a local ranch.

"This is the Ben and Sarah Crenshaw place," Poole said, reining his horse towards the ranch. "I know these people. It might be a good idea to stop and ask them if they have seen four strangers pass this way."

"Perhaps we should warn them too, Braxton, since they're friends of yours."

"I didn't say they were friends; I said I know them."

Olsen thought it was a strange response, coming from Poole. Now he was suddenly curious about what would make Poole say such a thing, something so out of character for the man he knew.

"What did that mean?"

"Nothing, Miles. Let it be."

"Why should I?" he asked.

"You're not going to let this go, are you?"

Olsen shook his head. "Not for one minute."

"You damn busybody. You're worse than a woman."

Miles laughed. "I'm half woman. My mother was a woman."

Olsen was relentless on things such as this. Poole knew his only chance to shut Miles' mouth was for him to fully explain.

"I've known Sarah Crenshaw long before she became Sarah Crenshaw. Her parents were good friends of mine," he explained, drawing rein not too far from the ranch. "Her parents didn't much like Ben Crenshaw and disapproved of his interest in their only daughter. About three years ago, both of her parents died when their home was caught ablaze."

"A fire killing both parents, that was convenient."

"I thought so too. But what I believed and what I could prove were two vastly different things. The two of them are married now."

"Is that all?"

"I wish it was, Miles. Not only is Ben Crenshaw a drunk; the man is a mean drunk. Rumor has it that he beats Sarah," Poole continued. "The bruises she tries to hide lend a passel of credibility to the rumors. To make a long story short, I truly like Sarah Crenshaw. She deserves much better than what she's got. And her little boy, he reminds me a lot of Adam. When it comes to Ben Crenshaw, I despise the vermin she has as a husband. Now, there, are you satisfied?"

Miles nodded. "I am now."

"Good, Miles. Can we finally get back to business?" he said, the easy smile leaving Poole's face almost as soon as it came. He pointed a finger towards the ranch yard. "Hey, what is that?"

Poole spurred his horse into a run, followed by Olsen, who was held back by his need to bring along the pack horse.

Upon riding up to the ranch, they immediately saw Jason Evers' body next to the well. Olsen and Poole drew their guns and dismounted next to the body. Seeing that his throat had been cut, the pair of lawmen went on high alert, in case any other dangers existed for them here.

"He dresses like a gambler," Poole said, fumbling through his saddle bags. "And there's a couple decks of cards here too."

"Look right here," Olsen said, pointing towards the tracks. "It had to be an Indian what done it. These prints were made by a set of moccasins."

"Yeah, it was an Indian, all right," Poole said, "A white man would have taken the saddle too."

Olsen continued puzzling over the tracks while Poole, six-gun in hand, sprinted towards the ranch house.

He paused beside the open door to let his eyes adjust to the change in lighting. He also noticed the bloody hand and footprints leading away. After a couple of seconds, Poole burst into the room, leading with his revolver. It was then he saw the bloodbath inside the tiny ranch house.

Once certain that there was nobody else in the ranch house besides him, Poole holstered his gun. He knelt beside the dead body of Ben Crenshaw and noticed the gun near his hand. He also found the knife wound in the man's back. The dead rancher's gun smelled like it had been fired recently. There was also a single spent cartridge in the cylinder. Closer observation revealed a bullet hole in the wall near the edge of the open door, like Ben had fired at someone entering the room suddenly.

That stranger, probably the dead man out by the well, had probably been the one to shoot Ben Crenshaw. Poole figured Ben's death was probably nothing more than a case of self-defense.

Poole guessed that the knife wound had been inflicted by someone close to him, a person Ben trusted, perhaps his wife, Sarah. That speculation was also helped along by the fact that Sarah was nowhere to be found here, and her son, Sam, was missing as well.

Due to her gentle nature, Poole couldn't picture Sarah ever harming anyone, let alone stabbing her husband. He puzzled over what Ben had finally done which would push the woman to ever commit such an uncharacteristic act of violence.

Poole knew it must have been serious.

It had been no secret to the locals, of course, that Ben and Sarah Crenshaw had suffered from a troubled marriage. Then there were the bruises the wife sometimes exhibited, which Sarah generally explained away as normal mishaps of ranch life. Those occasional bruises only served to fuel the rumors, stories that Ben had been beating and abusing his wife.

In talking to others, Marshal Poole routinely dismissed those accusations as little more than idle gossip, but in reality, he didn't really doubt them. The events that transpired in this room, however, convinced Poole that his suspicions, and his opinions, were indeed correct.

Ben Crenshaw was a pathetic little man who beat his wife and society wouldn't be at all harmed by his departure.

"Good Lord. What happened in here?" Olsen said, while framed in the doorway.

The sudden remark startled Marshal Poole, who clawed for his gun and pointed it towards the door.

Olsen threw up his hands in surrender. "Calm down, Braxton. It's just me."

Looking a little sheepish, Poole returned the gun to his holster. "Sorry about that, Miles. I guess that story you told me about the Willards and the deaths which just happened here have got me a little jumpy."

"The kid outside was named Jason Evers. I found a couple of letters addressed to him in his coat," Olsen said. "His gun had one spent cartridge. He was also carrying a right tidy sum of cash."

"Did the letters give any clue as to where his relatives might be located?"

"Yes, they did. Evers has a sister in Chicago. I'll make sure she gets the money."

"Sounds good," Poole replied, before sharing his speculations about this incident with the other lawman, Olsen nodding at the details as Poole spoke.

"That makes sense," Miles replied. "It also goes along with what I found outside. Follow me, Braxton."

Poole tagged along as his friend went out the door. He watched as Olsen pointed at the tracks leading up to and away from the house. "This set of tracks, I think, belonged to the young fellow next to the well. He obviously came to the house, unaware of what already transpired inside."

Poole picked it up from there. "And once he went into the house, Crenshaw, already nursing a serious knife wound, took a shot at him. Crenshaw missed."

"But the kid sure didn't," Olsen added.

"No, he didn't at all. Might have been the only thing that saved Sarah from being considered a murderer. After getting stabbed like that, I can't believe Ben lasted long enough to get shot."

Olsen then proceeded to point out the other two sets of tracks, ones leading away from the ranch. "Here is where the woman left the house, probably taking her boy with him. And this is the place where the horse stood, when she was loading up the boy and their gear. It looks like Mrs. Crenshaw also used the porch to climb up on what I suspect to be a tall horse."

Poole rubbed his chin. "Maybe Sarah already thought Ben was dead, that she had killed him with the knife."

"Could be. In fact, it's real likely."

Once more, Olsen pointed at the ground. "Looky here," the lawman said. "This is the one set of tracks that really bothers me."

"Yeah," Poole replied. "There's that moccasin print again. That Indian is climbing onto his horse and leading an extra mount, which matches the print made by the gambler's horse earlier. I don't like this."

"Me neither," Miles said. "The Indian done took out after her, or it sure appears that way. What should we do, try to save the woman and her baby or forget about them and focus on bringing Metcalf and those other animals to justice?"

Poole shook his head. "It's a quandary that would make Solomon get liquored up. What do you think, Miles?"

"That decision's above my pay rate. You're the United States Marshal, Poole. I'll make do with whatever you decide. But if we help the woman first, I'm still going after Metcalf and his boys as soon as we're done."

Poole threw the reins up over his horse's neck and swung himself in the saddle. Olsen followed his lead.

"I guess we're in agreement then," Poole said. "We'll try to help Sarah."

"I reckon so," Olsen replied. "You think we should bury those bodies before we ride out of here?"

"Not now," Poole said. "I'm guessing Metcalf has got about a four to six hour start on us. There could be a whole passel of bodies that need burying if we don't get to moving right now."

Chapter Ten

The two marshals never spoke as they continued following the trail of Kicking Deer and Sarah Crenshaw. They made no sound except for the leather creaking on their saddles and the clicking of horseshoes against the dusty rocks.

After trailing them for almost a mile, Poole and Olsen saw where the Indian had veered off from the woman's trail and ridden off in another direction, leading Evers' horse behind him as he rode.

Olsen knelt down by the tracks and scratched his head at the strange turn of events. "This don't make any sense to me at all, Braxton. Why did he give up? The Indian knew the woman had to be an easy target. Why did he stop?"

Poole looked down from his horse and said, "It sure ain't the behavior of any Apache I've ever seen, especially with another good horse right there for the taking."

Olsen got up from the ground and climbed back on his saddle. "So, what now, Braxton? It looks like the woman isn't facing any immediate danger, not from this one brave anyway."

Poole removed his hat and scratched his head while he thought, before finally returning the hat to his head. "I don't see we have any other choice. Sarah Crenshaw isn't wanted for anything. She may have stabbed her husband, but with what I know about the man, Ben probably had it coming.

"We also know she inflicted a mortal wound on Crenshaw, but the knife wound wasn't ultimately responsible for his death. The law has no reason to apprehend her and it appears that she's in no immediate danger," he added. "Under those circumstances, Miles, it really only leaves us one thing to do. We have to get back on the trail of Metcalf and his men. Isn't that the way you see it too?"

"I already told you, Braxton. That decision is above my pay rate. But if you really care for my opinion, I think we need to get back to pursuing those outlaws."

"It's decided then. Lead the way, Miles."

* * *

Sarah Crenshaw continued riding, unsure of where she was headed. In the moment, she thought of nothing other than getting away and guaranteeing the safety of her son. Now that she was gone, Sarah wondered how long it would be before the authorities discovered that she stabbed her husband to death. And how soon would it be before the law came looking for her?

Unsure of why it really mattered to her at all, Sarah hoped that the arrest would not be conducted by Marshal Poole, the kind man who lost his wife and son.

"Where are we going, Mama?" Sam said.

"I'm not sure yet, but it will be a good home. A good, safe place for both of us."

"Will Papa be coming?"

"I don't think so, dear. Papa needs to get well first."

"Is he hurt?"

"Yes."

"I saw him hit you. Did it hurt?"

"Yes, he hurt me."

"I'm sorry you're hurt," he replied, wrapping his arms tighter around her waist than before.

"Thanks for worrying about me, dear, but I'm all better now. Mama will be fine, just so long as she has you here with her."

The boy said nothing further, leaning his head up against his mother for comfort.

For a young child, a mother's presence was often enough to satisfy him and quell his fears.

Unwavering trust in his mother brought comfort to the child, but Sarah believed the child's confidence in her was certainly misplaced. Increasingly, she was growing worried, fearful of where they would spend the night, where they would eventually live, and how she would support them if they were indeed fortunate to find a place.

There weren't a lot of jobs in the West for a woman alone, and many of those were not occupations that a decent woman would ever aspire to hold. But Sarah knew the future would wait. Nightfall was coming upon them soon and she desperately needed to find them a good place to sleep.

Sarah wasn't worried about being caught in the rain, because there had been no rainfall in over a month. Recently, there had barely been any remaining trace of dew on the ground come morning. If dew had fallen, the dusty ground lapped it up like a thirsty dog. A quick check of the sky revealed that there didn't appear to be any relief coming anytime soon to alleviate this endless drought.

The pair of lonely riders on horseback continued westward. Sarah knew they must find water soon, not only for them, but also for the horse which they rode.

Initially thinking the tiny structure that she saw off in the distance might have been her weary eyes playing tricks on her, Sarah paid it no mind. Yet as they rode closer, Sarah was certain it was a place the two of them could seek shelter for the night. Perhaps someone would be there to help them.

Any thoughts of help came and went as fast as she had them.

In the fading light of dusk, Sarah noticed there were no lights to be seen. Also, no smoke billowed from the chimney. The building was a decrepit, old line shack.

"Look, Mama," Sam said, pointing his finger off into the distance. "A house."

"I see it, dear."

As far as the worried mother was concerned, the tiny, abandoned line shack looked as inviting to her as would the finest Boston mansion. For the first time on this day, Sarah's face offered up a genuine smile, one filled with relief and thankfulness.

The place promised warmth and shelter to her and her son, making it unnecessary for them to sleep out on the ground. Perhaps the shack also had a bed inside, something on which they could catch a few precious hours of sleep.

Upon arriving at the shack, Sarah climbed down from her saddle and hitched the reins to a porch post. She now regretted her foolishness in failing to take Ben's revolver before she fled the house. The few items she brought were contained in a poke and tied to the saddle horn. It was then she remembered that she hadn't even considered what items might still be contained in Ben's saddle bags.

The only weapon Sarah had was her husband's rifle, which had been left upon the saddle when she fled the house.

She jacked a cartridge into the chamber and prepared to go inside.

"You stay here for now," she said to Sam, still seated on horseback.

"Yes, Mama."

"I'll make sure it's good and safe for us and then I will come back for you."

The boy nodded.

As she threw open the door, she saw a mouse go scrambling through a small hole next to the fireplace. Except for their tiny friend, the place was empty. Sarah cast one final look around at their dusty, yet wonderful accommodations.

Another smile came to her lips. It would do nicely for the two of them.

Leaning her rifle up against the wall, just inside the door, Sarah went back outside to join her son. After she lifted him down from the saddle, Sam ran inside the open door, curious to see what was inside.

A meager supply of firewood and kindling were stacked outside, leaning against the side of the shack. Sarah walked outside, followed by her son. She loaded up an armful of wood while Sam carried several of the smaller pieces for kindling. While waiting for the fire to take hold, Sarah found a tired broom and began sweeping away the months of dust and neglect.

The bed was little more than a creaky, wooden frame, covered by a battered mattress, chewed upon and used by their tiny friend for a nesting place. Yet Sarah knew it would serve them well as a restful spot for the evening, a condition much better than sleeping upon the ground all night long.

Not too long after Sarah had the place looking more respectable, a warm and comforting flame danced in the old fireplace. Next, she returned to the horse, retrieving her sack of provisions, along with her husband's saddle bags.

Remembering her father's admonitions about always taking time to care for their stock, Sarah was ashamed she didn't have any feed or water for the horse. And with the two of them still on the run, the woman didn't believe she could afford the luxury of removing the saddle from her mount. After several moments of agonizing over the decision, Sarah finally relented to loosen its cinch.

Once back in the shack, Sarah warmed the cold biscuits by placing them near the fire and prepared something to eat from the few items she snatched from her house.

As she nibbled on her now-lukewarm biscuit and watched the child eat, Sarah noticed he was strangely silent. It worried her because she was fearful about what the child might be thinking. She was also concerned, but a little uncertain of how much of the violence her son had witnessed back at their house. Sara longed to ask Sam about what he'd seen, but she was fearful that the questions might only stir painful memories that the child would be better off never to recall.

"I'm thirsty, Mama."

"I know it, Sam. I'll do my best to try to find you something to drink tomorrow. But for now, you need to eat to keep up your strength."

"Yes, Mama."

The boy finished eating and his mother put him to bed, kissing him lightly on the cheek and pulling the blanket over him for warmth. Softly, she sang to Sam for a few minutes as Sarah watched him drift off to sleep.

After taking care of her son, Sarah picked up her husband's saddlebags and moved a chair over next to the fire. Using the flames for light, she sat down and began to dig through their contents.

The woman was not surprised to learn there was a full bottle of whiskey right on top. She knew the liquor would do nothing to soothe her thirst, but Sarah couldn't resist the urge to remove the top and take a drink. The liquor burned all the way down. She then took another drink, concluding it didn't taste much better than the first. She replaced the lid on the bottle and set it down on the floor next to her.

At least the whiskey could be used for antiseptic, should either of them sustain any kind of a wound.

Digging deeper into the one bag, she found a knife, matches, and some extra cartridges. Underneath it all was a battered and neglected copy of the Scriptures that she once gave to Ben. A number of the pages were matted together, as a result of the whiskey droplets that often fell upon them, spilled by a drunken man swaying in the saddle. It wasn't hard to tell that King James ruled nothing in the realm of Ben Crenshaw.

In the other side of the bag, Sarah was pleased to discover that Ben had left an extra six-gun, cartridge belt, and holster, all rolled up inside. She removed the gun and checked to make sure it was properly loaded.

Sarah now believed that, along with her rifle, she might have a chance to keep the two of them protected. Except for the revolver and gun belt, along with the Bible, she returned the items to the saddlebags.

She tossed some more wood on the fire, before moving her chair closer to the fire for lighting. Longing for some comfort of her own, perhaps that which might come from above, Sarah opened up Ben's battered and neglected copy of the Scriptures and her eyes fell upon the second verse of Genesis.

"And the earth was without form, and void; and darkness was upon the face of the deep. And the Spirit of God moved upon the face of the waters."

Waters.

Sarah closed the book and softly breathed a desperate prayer, asking that the same Spirit of God would somehow smile down upon the two of them and guide her to the face of those waters.

She went over to the bed and glanced down at her sleeping son. Sarah lightly touched his face and climbed underneath the covers next to Sam. His sleepy body stirred and he snuggled closer to his mother.

Sarah held his small body against her bosom, as her lonely and fearful eyes filled with tears.

Chapter Eleven

The sun still wasn't visible when Lefty Pitts opened his eyes. The barely flickering light of a waning fire was just enough to break up some of the darkness. He looked around the camp and saw that none of the others had begun stirring yet. Lefty's mouth was dry and he was still suffering the ill effects of last night's liquor.

As bad as he desired a cup of coffee, he first needed to relieve himself. Struggling to unwind himself from the knotted bedroll and to make it up on his feet, Lefty didn't even take time to pull his pants up over his long johns, before staggering outside the camp in his sock feet. He climbed a small hillside and undid his fly. Standing in front of a tree, he grunted in pain as he let out water upon the dry tree bark.

Despite his hangover, he still had the presence of mind not to piss against the wind. As the yellow stream marked the base of the tree, Lefty's nose caught the hint of wood smoke. At first, he thought it may have been their own fire, but Lefty knew their camp was located in the direction he was facing. This scent of smoke was upwind, coming from behind him.

Lefty finished his business and ambled down the hill to investigate.

He carefully moved through the trees, fearful of stubbing his toe. Lefty cursed himself for failing to pull on his boots.

The first dim rays of sunshine were just starting to appear in the sky as he saw the form of the small line shack. Lefty softly cussed himself once again, for failing to take his knife or a gun with him before leaving the camp. He also longed to have his pants.

The outlaw carefully inched his way around the front of the shack, seeing no light coming from inside the structure, with nothing but the chimney smoke to alert anyone of the building's presence.

Then Lefty saw the horse.

With only one horse outside, he figured there probably wouldn't be more than a single person inside. But Lefty also knew he was unarmed, a condition likely not shared by whoever was sleeping inside the shack. He considered trying to peer in through the window glass, but he finally decided to exercise caution while alone.

Lefty Pitts had never been praised for his thinking skills, but the outlaw excelled at random larceny. He decided the horse was simply there for the taking. It would require no great time or effort to ride back to his camp, get the others, and return to the line shack to rob the person or persons inside.

He slipped up to the house, and moving quietly as possible, untied the horse from the porch. As Lefty placed his foot in the stirrup and started to swing himself into the saddle, the loosened cinch made the saddle rotate off the horse's back, dumping the bewildered outlaw onto his back in the dirt.

"Dammit," he muttered.

Lefty was even more surprised to look up from the ground and see a woman's face, an attractive woman, holding a rifle on him. He started to explain his actions and get up from the ground, but before he could begin to formulate a reasonable lie or make any effort to protect himself, the woman clubbed Lefty alongside his head with the steel of her rifle barrel.

The outlaw was caught completely off guard by the woman and the violence of her sudden actions.

The rifle blow rattled Lefty's skull and knocked him unconscious, leaving him in darkness until the sun climbed much higher in the eastern sky.

* * *

Surprised she slept as soundly as she did, Sarah Crenshaw opened her eyes to see it was still dark outside. Since the last time she added wood, the flames had dwindled down to merely embers. The coals offered them little heat and provided almost no lighting to the room.

Fearful of waking Sam, she worked at gathering their things together in the darkness. Knowing the two of them might have to leave at a moment's notice, Sarah had deliberately kept their belongings close at hand.

As she was almost done with her preparations to leave, Sarah thought she heard something outside. Her first impulse was that the resident mouse had returned, but then Sarah heard the same sound again. She also knew her eyes had, since she rose from her slumber, adjusted to the darkness around her. Sarah saw absolutely no movement inside the line shack. Freezing in place, she listened and waited.

Then she heard it again.

Somebody was outside; she was sure of it.

Sarah caught up the rifle and softly eared back the hammer, moving towards the door to investigate. She was confident she also saw the silhouette of a man moving in front of the window. The figure crept away from the window and she heard him inching towards their horse.

Taking a deep breath and mouthing a silent prayer, she gently and slowly opened the door, standing in the open doorway with her rifle ready to fire. The man had no idea of her presence or her close proximity to him. Sarah saw the stranger's back was to her, as he tried to swing himself into the saddle.

Just before she ordered the would-be horse thief to halt, the loosened cinch gave way, dumping the man onto his back. When the stunned stranger looked up from his place there on the ground, their eyes met.

Without saying a word, or allowing him the opportunity to say something as well, Sarah struck Lefty Pitts in the head with her rifle barrel.

When Sarah was sure he was unconscious, she dashed back inside the line shack. She buckled her husband's gun belt around her hips, retrieved a knife and a couple of short pieces of rope that looked like something her daddy called, "piggin' strings."

She used the strings to bind the stranger's ankles and wrists. Fearful the bonds wouldn't be enough to slow the man down, should he manage to untie himself, Sarah cut the long johns free from his body and tossed the shredded garments on the ground next to him. She even took his socks, cutting them to rags as well.

Sarah knew it was unlikely this man came all this way in his socks and long johns, without a horse. She figured his camp had to be someplace nearby. She also reasoned that if he had a camp, then there would likely be others with him.

Alone and likely outnumbered, Sarah knew they must leave immediately.

Moving with the efficiency of a seasoned military general, Sarah tightened the cinch on her saddle, loaded their belongings, and finally grabbed her sleeping child. In less than ten minutes, the two of them were riding away from the old line shack. She held the sleepy child close in front of her, casting one final look back into the distance, at the bound, naked, and unconscious outlaw, on the ground behind them, the first rays of dawn appearing on the eastern skies.

Recalling the current condition of the horse thief, and her part in the events that left Pitts starkly helpless, she grudgingly acknowledged her reaction wouldn't be considered proper behavior for a lady.

Still, Sarah couldn't help but smile, leaving the unconscious outlaw behind her.

* * *

The sun was already high in the sky when the outlaws rode down to see what happened to Lefty Pitts.

"What the hell happened to you?" Hank Metcalf said, looking down at his friend.

"Some damn snip of a woman."

"You're saying a woman did this to you?" Bill Ford asked.

"Yeah, busted me right across the noggin with her rifle, she did. It was right after I tried to steal her horse."

"You're naked as a fresh sprout from the womb," Hank said, still on horseback. "Tied up like a calf for branding. You might want to get some clothes on, son, before you get an ugly burn on your privates."

Lefty Pitts let out with a vicious string of profanities, aimed at the three riders gathered around him. "I might be able to get dressed if one of you damn fools would climb down from those saddles and untie me."

"Why'd you come down here naked?" one of them said.

"I didn't come down here naked. I had my long johns on."

"That's still pretty much naked," Russell said with a smile.

"That woman done this to me," he nodded his head over towards a pile of shredded long johns. "She cut them off of me. Took my damn socks too. I guess she wanted to make it hard for me to follow her."

Sid Russell started laughing, leaning one elbow on the saddle horn. "Hey, Hank, you don't suppose she acted upon her womanly urges with Lefty while he was sleeping, do you?"

Metcalf joined him in the joke. "You might be on to something."

"Yeah, Lefty," Russell added, "she done taken away your virtue while you were fast asleep. Sort of had her way with you, smoked a cigarette, and rode off."

Metcalf couldn't resist lending his part to his partner's further misery. "Tell me, Lefty, how's it feel to be violated against your will?"

"Shut up, Hank."

"From what I can see," Ford said, "there ain't enough evidence that Lefty could ever do a woman much good at all."

Upon hearing Ford's comment, the three mounted outlaws broke into another few moments of raucous laughter.

"I swear if you don't hurry up and get me untied, I'm gonna take my knife and cut every damn one of your heads off and piss down your necks."

Hank smiled. "Not if your thing's too burned by the sun to touch it, you won't. All right, Bill. Cut him loose. And you be damn careful with that blade. We don't have need for any steers."

Ford cast a doubtful eye down at the naked outlaw and spat a green stream of tobacco into the dust beside his head. "I sure didn't join up with you boys for this," Bill said, reluctantly climbing down from his saddle to cut Pitts free from the ropes.

"Sid, let him share your horse, long enough for us to go back to camp for his things."

"Not until Pitts gets some damn clothes on," said Russell. "I ain't riding double with no naked man."

"You boys wait here," Ford said, forking his saddle. "I'll head back up to camp and gather Lefty's gear. Besides," he said, looking down at Pitts and once more spitting into the dust near Lefty's bare feet, "I've already seen more of him than I care to."

"Hurry back, Bill," Hank said, climbing down from horseback. "We've already wasted enough time today. And you go and cover yourself up with whatever's left of them long johns, Lefty, and we'll do some palavering until Ford comes back. Besides, I'm dying to know how a lone woman got the drop on a vicious killer like you."

Rubbing his sore wrists, Lefty walked over and gathered what was left of his long johns and attempted to cover himself with the tattered remainder. "That was one fine horse the woman was riding. I might have had it too, if not for her loosening the cinch."

"That explains why you were on the ground long enough for her to hit you," Hank said, leading his horse over towards the shack. Sid Russell dismounted and followed him. "Man ought to always check the cinch."

Lefty fumbled with the ragged garments, thinking he'd do a much better job clothing himself with only a set of fig leaves. "Well, you can bet I plan on cutting out that whore's filthy tongue if I ever see her again."

"Good," Hank said, tying his mount to the porch rail. He glanced back towards Bill's trail and saw that his horse disappeared into the hills. "Until Ford comes back, we can go inside and talk about that idea too."

Chapter Twelve

Three hours after leaving the Crenshaw ranch, Olsen and Poole picked up the four outlaws' trail. Poole was a capable tracker, but he was nearly speechless while watching Miles work. Despite the marshal's shortcomings with a gun, Olsen was like an Apache on the trail.

Poole didn't even bother to dismount when Olsen stopped to check signs. Braxton was wise enough to step aside and let a master work. Poole knew he was far better suited to keep his gun handy and cover them from trouble while Olsen devoted his attention to deciphering the trail.

It wasn't that he could simply read the signs of what they had done, Olsen also had a knack for knowing what they might do next, where they would go, and why they would do it. In a sense, Miles almost transformed himself into those individuals he was hunting.

After the atrocities Hank Metcalf visited upon his friends, the Willard family, Miles Olsen had grown obsessed with catching up with the outlaws and seeing they paid for their crimes. Marshal Olsen was also aware that Metcalf's gang was at least four to six hours ahead of them. Determined to make up those hours, Olsen grew relentless, refusing to eat or even take time to get a drink of water from his canteen.

Marshal Poole feared what that kind of hatred might do to a man. He'd seen it before in others; he'd experienced those same feelings himself. Yet the longer he rode and the more Olsen told him stories about the generosity and kindness of Anse Willard and his family, the more devoted Poole became to embracing Olsen's cause.

Poole already was familiar with the vicious crimes of Bill Ford and knew the man would never again be taken alive. He figured it was likely that Ford had aligned himself with these other deadly and desperate outlaws, men who probably also shared his same notions about returning to prison.

Another few hours down the trail, the two marshals no longer held singular goals. Poole had adopted precisely the same mindset as his friend. Their connection certainly wasn't spoken or discussed between them. They just became a pair of men, united in an unholy mission to end the evil slaughter of the innocent souls which dwelt amongst them.

To hell with their badges, the laws they represented, and oaths they swore to uphold. Poole and Olsen knew these men must be stopped, by any manner necessary. That is what they dedicated themselves to do.

They would hunt these outlaws and murderers down and kill them where they stood. It was also mutually understood that the two men would never talk about it in the days to come and they would share no remorse over their actions in their waning years upon this earth.

Their quest was no longer a righteous one, but a few righteous ones might live to see another sunrise because of it.

Poole drew rein on the edge of the slope, which granted them a wide and open view of the landscape ahead of them. "What do you suggest we do now, Miles? It's getting dark. You want to catch a couple hours sleep and then try to get back on their trail?'

Olsen glared at him for a time while his horse continued walking. "Look, I've been thinking about this for the past couple miles, Braxton. We already know they have a lead on us. I wouldn't suggest this to a lesser man, but I know you're capable of it. That's why I came to get you. Our only hope to make up those critical hours is to ride harder, longer, and faster than Metcalf. Are you willing to do that?"

"You know I am, Miles. But what about holding to their trail. Can you do it in the dark, only by matchlight?"

Olsen laughed. "You've seen me do it before, ain't you?"

Poole smiled. "But I also remember that one time, those lit matches in the darkness told them exactly where they needed to shoot. It almost got us killed."

"I never said it was a perfect plan."

"No, you sure didn't."

"But you have to admit that it worked. And besides, it only happened that one time twenty years ago."

"That doesn't really make me feel any better about it, Miles. Lucky their shooting didn't measure up to their bragging. Yeah, I'm with you on this one. Guess that makes me as crazy as you." Braxton reached into his coat pocket and pulled out a couple of pieces of jerked venison. He tasted one piece and handed the other one to Olsen. "These men have to be stopped. Maybe we can find them by morning. Here's hoping we both don't get ourselves killed in the process."

"I knew I could count on you," Olsen said, gnawing off a piece of the meat. "You know what they say, no guts, no glory."

Poole laughed without humor. "I'm thinking there won't be any glory for anyone on this hunt, Miles. Just guts . . . no glory."

For the next couple of hours they rode on, keeping their conversations to a minimum for their own safety. Their only stops would be to check the trail by matchlight and to dig another bite of the jerked meat from their saddlebags.

Approximately every twenty to thirty minutes, Olsen would draw rein, climb down from his saddle, and study the ground.

Had someone never seen his boundless skills as a tracker, they might have believed Olsen to be mad, following nothing in the darkness except his own imagination. Often, his study of the ground revealed nothing, in those moments relying mostly on his own intuition and an intimate knowledge of a wanted man's behavior.

Poole had seen his friend in action a number of times. Yet despite his knowledge of Olsen's remarkable skill on the trail, the United States Marshal never ceased to marvel at his abilities.

Knowing he was no match for Olsen's abilities as a manhunter, Poole let Olsen take the lead on studying the trail. When there were no obvious signs, Olsen was also wise enough to discuss his hunches with Poole, talking over his theories with a fellow lawman, about what the outlaws might be thinking or doing, things which made it easier to figure where they might ultimately be headed next.

Of course, it was obvious to both of them, with this unbearable heat, that the outlaws would soon need to replenish their stores of water, the one critical necessity that all living beings, good or evil, shared.

Despite being a couple of hours before sunrise, with their world still shrouded by a blanket of heavy darkness, neither of the riders had experienced any relief from the heat. The bitter warmth had not relented with the departure of the sun. And with no hint of rain to be seen, the coming day promised more of the same harsh temperatures.

But for the pair of exhausted marshals, the unbearable heat from a soon-to-be rising sun was the least of their worries.

As Olsen extinguished the match and remounted, he looked over at Poole and softly spoke, "I think we're only about an hour behind them, Braxton. We'll have to take some extra caution now."

Poole stopped to check the loads in his guns. Once satisfied, he holstered the revolver and returned the rifle to the scabbard. Shaking his head, he said, "As many times as I've been on the trail with you, Miles, I still don't know how you do that."

"Lots of practice," Miles replied, verifying his guns were ready as well. He mopped the sweat from his forehead on his sleeve. "Let's get this done, Braxton, and go find ourselves a cool watering hole, just to plop our tired backsides in."

"Right behind you," Poole said, reining his horse around to follow his friend. "I'd almost sell my soul for a cup of hot coffee right now," he muttered under his breath to nobody in particular.

* * *

Riding back to their camp, Ford was swearing underneath his breath, angry for the trouble that Lefty's stupid behavior had caused them. They should have been gone at sunrise, had it not been for Pitts' foolhardy decision to go traipsing around the territory in the dark, adorned in nothing but his socks and long johns.

Ford also had several choice profanities for Hank Metcalf, whose failure to take a stern hand with Pitts led to these same kinds of reckless and repeated setbacks. Bill feared Pitts was likely to get them killed someday, unless Ford were to kill Hank and take over the outfit.

Once back to their camp, Bill stepped down from his horse, leaving his mount ground-tied as he went about his business. He made no effort to kick any dirt upon their fire, because he was solely focused on nothing other than gathering Lefty's saddle, bedroll, and horse. Every one of his movements was regimented, a product of his many years on the wrong side of the law, which often necessitated hasty departures from the many locations in which they made camp.

Catching up the bedroll and gear in his left hand and under the crook of his arm, Ford hoisted the saddle over his right shoulder and toted it over to Pitts' horse. Dropping the bedroll on the ground next to him, Bill blanketed the animal and lifted the saddle into place. He grabbed the stirrup on his side, hanging it over the horn while he cinched down the leather. A couple of moments later, he lashed down Lefty's bedroll behind the saddle and was ready to return down off the hill to where his friends waited.

Satisfied with the job now completed, Bill rolled a smoke, lit the end of it, and started leading the animal back to his own mount. Then he experienced a moment which was all too familiar to an outlaw. A slight glint of sunlight against steel caught his eye and he instinctively ducked as the slug lanced away the top of Ford's right ear.

Startled by the sudden gun shot, Ford's untethered horse went racing down over the hill, stirrups slapping wildly against its side.

Ford's first impulse to go racing after his own horse was instantly halted by an even stronger impulse to remain alive. He swung into Lefty's saddle and spurred the mount downhill, away from his pursuers, ducking low in his saddle while clawing for his six-gun to return fire.

Blood began to flow from the wound and a couple of the droplets blew into his right eye, making it difficult to see.

The former stillness of an early morning sunrise was broken by the sounds of galloping horses and the hostile blasts of gunfire.

Chapter Thirteen

It was the skilled and relentless tracking of Miles Olsen throughout the night that brought them in range of Metcalf's gang, but it was Braxton Poole's nose that alerted the determined pursuers that they had finally closed the gap.

The two riders had been riding in single file, which lessened any risks from the other horse marring the outlaws' trail.

Fearful that a shout might betray their position, Poole spurred his horse from behind until he rode abreast of Olsen. Poole reached over to touch the marshal's arm. "Do you smell that, Miles?"

Miles reined in his horse. "Smell? What?"

"Smoke from a fire. It's somewhere close."

"I smell it now," Olsen said with a smile.

Poole removed his hat and scratched his head. "You think it's them?"

"It has to be Metcalf. I can feel it."

"Quiet, slow, and careful," Poole said. "Maybe we can catch them off-guard."

"You don't know Metcalf," Olsen said. "He never drops his guard. If it's them, forget about the law and any of your ideas about fair play. Let's make sure we fire our first warning shots right into their damn skulls."

The pair of lawmen reined their horses downhill, riding in the direction of the wind. Only moments later, they saw the first, small tendrils of smoke, rising above the dwindling flames. Then they also smelled a cigarette, followed by glimpsing a lone man carrying a saddle to a second horse.

A look of disappointment swept across Olsen's face as he decided perhaps this individual wasn't part of the ones they were tracking.

The marshal's spirits lifted again when he saw Poole stop to shoulder his rifle. "That's Bill Ford."

Knowing he couldn't match Poole's skills with a Winchester, Olsen looped the pack horse's reins around his saddle horn. He pulled the rifle from his scabbard and eased his animals closer to camp, always making sure he didn't place him or his pair of horses anywhere between the lawman's gun and the outlaw.

Waiting as long as he dared, all the while hoping and praying Olsen could get close enough to take out at least one of the others, Poole held his breath and began to take up slack on the trigger. In the split second he expected to witness Ford's skull explode like an overripe melon, the outlaw's head moved.

Knowing he should have aimed for his body, Poole mouthed a foul oath as he realized his slug just missed, clipping the outlaw's ear. He saw a spray of blood from the wound. Poole ejected the spent shell and chambered another, the sounds coming as nearly one. Then he fired a second time, this one hitting the fleeing outlaw in the left shoulder, marking the back of his shirt in a splotch of vivid crimson.

Off to Poole's right, he could hear Olsen opening fire on the outlaw with his long gun and Ford's six-gun answering theirs with a couple futile blasts of his own. The wounded Ford spurred Pitts' horse into a run, racing away for cover and hoping to rejoin his friends before these unknown lawmen caught up with them.

Poole, keeping his rifle cradled in his arm, spurred his horse into a dead run. He was determined to keep Ford in sight, confident the outlaw would soon be linking up with the others, somewhere nearby.

Miles shouted after him, but Poole saw and heard nothing but the outlaw's horse, fleeing the marshals' guns. As much as Olsen wanted to break into a gallop, it was impossible with the weighted-down pack horse in tow. But as he passed through the camp, the signs were unmistakable. He knew Metcalf's gang had been here, all of them, only minutes earlier.

At this moment, the man most obsessed with killing these outlaws was no longer Miles Olsen. With his first glance of the murderer and rapist, Bill Ford, Poole became the driven lawman, with absolutely no interest in bringing these men to justice. Marshal Poole was *only* determined to bring justice to them.

From the sounds of the gunfire, Ford figured he wasn't being pursued by a full posse. He surmised there weren't more than two or three lawmen in the bunch who were shooting at him. Bill guessed one of them to be Miles Olsen, the town marshal, whose jurisdiction wasn't too far away from where he raped and killed that handsome, golden haired Willard woman.

Even while running away from these lawmen bent on killing him, Ford couldn't help but smile at the memory of twice violating Anse Willard's wife, with only Metcalf passing on his own turn with the woman, before the horror and violence of their actions left her still and unable to speak.

But for now, Ford knew there would be other times, other women. Although Pitts' horse wasn't nearly as good as his own, it still ran well. Bill knew his wounds wouldn't kill him and neither would these marshals, not if they were fool enough to miss their first shot.

If he could reach the others only a few moments before Olsen and the others caught up with him, Ford figured that his guns, combined with those of Hank and Sid, might be enough to turn the tables on their pursuers.

Bill didn't even consider Lefty Pitts into the equation, because he had every intention of killing the man himself.

Bitter Water

* * *

Upon hearing the shooting on the hill above them, Hank Metcalf and Sid Russell ran outside of the line shack and mounted their horses. Their guns were in their hands, ready for trouble, wondering how long they should dare wait for Bill's return.

While they listened to the shooting above them and waited, Lefty Pitts stood naked on the line shack's porch, hoping nothing happened to Ford, who was supposed to be bringing his horse and gear, along with his needed clothes.

At that moment they saw Ford's horse running past them, saddle empty. The animal never slowed down and disappeared into the distance.

"Come on boys. Let's get out of here," Hank said. "They must have got Ford."

The words had no more left his lips when they heard another surge of gunfire and another horse galloping their way. Bill was riding Pitts' horse. Even from a distance Metcalf could tell it was Ford and that he had been wounded.

Ford drew rein next to the others. "Not much time to decide, Hank. We're going to have to either run or fight. There are two or three marshals up there. They're coming this way, fast."

"You hurt bad?"

"No, I'll live."

Anxious and fearful that the gang would leave him behind, Pitts ran out to where Ford was sitting his horse. "You have my gear?"

"I ought to kill you, Pitts. You're the reason I lost my own mount," Ford said, tossing Lefty's full canteen, bedroll, and saddle bags into the dust.

The naked Pitts squatted down next to his gear and began rifling through it for his clothes, boots, and gun belt. Lefty found the gun before he located his pants.

"Can't one of you let me ride double?"

Nobody responded to the naked outlaw's plea.

"Bill's horse just ran past here. If we can catch it and if you can hold out until then, we'll come back for you," Hank lied.

"You're not going to leave me here to be arrested by those marshals, are you?" Pitts asked.

The outlaw's question was never answered as Braxton Poole came racing down the hillside, the marshal's buckskin hot on Ford's tail. Poole's gun started raining fire down upon them.

The three outlaws began returning fire of their own, forcing Poole to seek some cover from the superior numbers. Once he was finally joined by Olsen, the lawmen resumed the fight. One of Poole's shots creased Hank's side, just below the right armpit.

The gunshot wound was more than enough to convince Metcalf that the time for fighting was over and fleeing would now be the wisest course of action.

Metcalf wasted no time in reining his horse around and spurring the mare into a run. Following closely behind him were the other two outlaws, leaving the line shack a distant memory.

Knowing he was left alone, Pitts only had time to snatch up his gun belt and go sprinting for the safety of the empty line shack. Almost reaching the tiny structure, Lefty snapped off a good shot as he ran. The slug barely missed Poole, knocking loose the hat from the marshal's head.

Poole returned his fire, hitting nothing. His next slug, fired from a wild gallop, caught the bandit squarely in the chest, knocking the naked outlaw off his feet and into the dirt.

His body came to rest only three feet from the structure's porch.

Despite the severity of his mortal injury, Pitts scrambled for his dropped pistol, his actions thwarted when Poole dismounted and kicked it away from his hand. By that time, Poole was joined by his friend, Olsen, and the other outlaws had disappeared from sight.

Poole was still enraged that Ford had once more escaped. "I would have killed Ford if not for your interference. Now, I'll kill you."

Poole drew his six-gun, pointed it at Pitts' head, and was already taking up slack on the trigger. Olsen stepped forward, grabbed his friend's gun hand, and pulled it down towards the ground.

"Don't bother, Braxton. He's only got a few minutes left."

From the location of the wound and with no clothing to conceal its severity, there were no doubts in anyone's mind that the man's time on this earth would indeed be short. Olsen clearly wanted these men dead, but he had no real words to console a dying man during his final moments on this side of eternity.

Despite his earlier rage and obsession to catch these men, Olsen knew his own bout with madness had passed. Of course, he still knew these outlaws wouldn't be stopped without being killed, but not like this.

Olsen was also bewildered by the actions of his friend. After their many instances of trailing outlaws together, he had never seen this side of Poole before. Even the sudden deaths of his wife and son hadn't brought this dark side of the marshal's nature to the surface.

Looking up from the ground, Pitts smiled at the two lawmen. "What's the matter? You never seen a naked man before?"

Poole wanted answers. "What's your name, mister?"

"Lefty Pitts." The dying outlaw coughed suddenly, spitting up small bubbles of frothy blood. "You got anything to drink?"

Olsen went over to his horse and removed a partial bottle of whiskey from his saddlebags. As he walked over towards the outlaw, Poole held Olsen back. "We already know about Bill Ford and Hank Metcalf. Not one damn drop until he tells us who else was with him."

"Sid, it was Sid Russell."

Poole nodded and released his firm grip on the other marshal's arm. Olsen made a strange face at his friend before moving. He knelt down next to Pitts, raised his head, and helped the man take a couple of small swigs from the bottle.

"That there's some fine whiskey. Olsen, is it?"

"Yeah, I'm Miles Olsen," he replied, throwing a nod in the direction of Poole. "And this here hombre is U.S. Marshal Braxton Poole." Pitts nodded in a look of recognition. "Heard of you, both of you. Figured the law might get me someday, but I never thought I'd die like this. It was that blame woman what got me killed."

Poole's eyes grew large at the statement. "Woman, you say?"

Upon hearing what Pitts said, Olsen moved over towards the line shack and began studying the other tracks. Even while he began analyzing the signs, Olsen's ear was still listening for anything else the dying outlaw might reveal as to what happened here at this line shack before their arrival.

"Yeah, some good-looking woman was sleeping in the shack when I tried to steal her horse." Pitts coughed a couple of times before continuing to speak. "I would have gotten away clean if she hadn't loosened the cinch on her saddle."

Olsen was still kneeling on one knee as he said, "The tracks definitely belong to Mrs. Crenshaw, Braxton."

"Hit me with her rifle, she did. Then she took my damn clothes too."

Poole couldn't help but smile, pleased that Mrs. Crenshaw was still unharmed.

"Yes, sir," Lefty said, "never figured on this one."

It was the last statement Pitts would ever make, the outlaw leaving this world adorned in the same fashions in which he entered it.

Olsen walked back over to Poole to share with him the information he learned from studying the tracks, combined with the details he gleaned from the outlaw's story. One glance told him that Pitts was already dead.

"We've got another problem, Marshal," Olsen said, removing his hat to wipe his sweaty brow. "The Crenshaw woman . . ."

Poole never let the marshal finish his sentence. "Yeah, Miles, I know. Sarah Crenshaw has no idea that there are three rapists and mankillers riding hard on the trail behind her and her son."

Olsen shook his head. "This gets more complicated by the moment."

Yeah," Poole said, "and I'm still wondering what became of that damned Indian."

Chapter Fourteen

A troubled Sarah Crenshaw rode across the barren landscape, aimlessly searching for some sign of water.

"I'm thirsty, Mama."

"I know it, Sam," she said. "I'll find you some water before nightfall."

Sarah knew her statement was a lie, but she didn't have the heart to tell her son anything else. As their need for water grew more serious, Sarah feared that her impetuous actions at home hadn't only killed her husband; her actions might also be responsible for needlessly killing her own child.

Their weary horse plodded onward, driven only by an inner need to serve the ones who rode upon her back.

As Sarah continued riding, the scenery appeared strangely familiar to her, as if she had traveled this way in the past. For a time, she just dismissed the notion as a figment of her imagination, probably brought on by her parched condition.

Two hours later, Sarah was startled to realize that she knew exactly the trail to water and the horse no longer wandered on its own.

After her mind searched through dozens of old names and memories, it finally came to her . . .

Daddy called it "Webster Springs."

Sarah's vision of the land had rekindled the embers of a distant memory in her mind. Her certainty came from recalling a journey she took with her father many years earlier, when she came West with her mother.

At that time, her father was a general in the Army and Apache attacks were much more commonplace for the territory. The soldiers escorted Sarah and her mother to his latest military post. During their journey, the soldiers stumbled upon this oasis in the middle of nowhere.

Even if Sarah was wrong, there could be no turning back now.

Only death awaited the pair.

She had already ridden farther away from her home than what she believed to be the distance to her nearest source of water. Nothing waited for Sarah Crenshaw at home but the body of her dead husband and quite possibly the law, waiting to catch up with a wife and mother who stabbed her own husband to death.

For Sarah Crenshaw, there were no good options, but for the two thirsty riders, their problems were only growing.

Sarah had no idea of the danger that lurked only mere miles behind her, men riding hard on horseback, dangerous men, also in need of water.

* * *

"A damn shame, it is," Poole said, shaking his head and stooping down to pick something off the ground.

"You mean about us having to kill Pitts?"

"No, Miles, that wasn't a shame. Another one of them dead is a blessing," Poole replied, holding up the wrecked item. "It's too bad Lefty's canteen was crushed and destroyed underneath my horse's hoof. We could have used that water." The lawman flung the worthless canteen back into the dust. "If we don't get to water soon, we'll be deader than he is."

Marshal Olsen gazed upward at another set of barren clouds and a relentless, blazing sun that offered no promise of surrender. There would be no relief from their thirst coming from the skies anytime soon. He knew their only hope of survival would be to find water.

A quick glance at his friend revealed that Poole was thinking the same thing, his face also directed towards the sky. "How far do you suppose it is to Webster Springs, Miles?"

"Several hours ride, I suppose."

"I guess we'd better be going then."

Olsen appeared to ignore his comment, walking towards the line shack as if he failed to hear Poole speak. "Where are you going?" Poole said.

"I'm looking for something to dig a grave." Olsen replied.

"Let it go."

"Let it go? You mean we're not going to bury Pitts either?"

"No, we aren't. We don't have time," Poole replied.

"Even the dregs of society, like this man, deserve a Christian burial."

"Normally I'd agree with you, Miles, but not today."

Olsen wheeled around and strode up to Poole, face-to-face, until their toes nearly met. His eyes locked on Poole's. Miles contemplated hitting his friend, just to jar him back to some sense of reason.

"Are you suggesting that we just leave him out here for the buzzards?"

"No, I'm just saying we leave his body out here. The buzzards are free to do whatever they choose."

"That's mighty hard of you, Braxton."

"Not as hard as it will be on Mrs. Crenshaw and her son if we don't catch up with those outlaws," Poole said. "Could you face living with the needless death of that good woman and her boy? Is that something you'd want on your conscience, Miles?"

"Of course not."

"I didn't think so," Poole said, catching up his reins and forking his saddle. He glared down at his friend from atop his saddle. "Are you coming?"

Olsen took one final glance back at the unclothed body of Lefty Pitts, once a man, but now only a corpse that would soon begin to bloat in the afternoon sun. Miles cast one final look upward, a hostile stare for the one on horseback. "Yes, I'm coming."

Once back in the saddle, Olsen spurred his horse into a trot until he rode up alongside Poole's buckskin.

Upon seeing him there, Poole said, "There's one other thing."

"Yeah, Braxton, what is it?"

"Don't you dare ever walk up on me like that again."

* * *

To a casual observer, the trio of tired horses appeared to have no direction, as if they aimlessly plodded along in single file. The three outlaws riding those mounts reeked of last night's whiskey and stale sweat.

The men were hot, thirsty, and miserable. One of them was unharmed. Two of them were nursing a wound of some kind. All three of them stunk and needed a bath. Yet despite their differences, they were united on only one thing other than their bad smell . . .

They all wanted to live.

And living meant they must find water.

As soon as the outlaws placed a safe distance between them and their pursuers, Hank ordered the others to slow their horses to a walk. Metcalf speculated that his pursuers were hampered by their need to bring along a pack horse.

Russell reached into his pocket, cut off a plug of tobacco, and shoved it in his jaw before speaking, "Do you figure they got Lefty, boss?"

"I'd bet my last dollar he returned to his maker naked and bootless."

The three outlaws all joined in a hearty laugh.

Pleased to finally be rid of the outlaw he always thought was a detriment to their trade, Bill Ford observed, "I'll bet Pitts is deader than that rancher you throwed that loop on, Sid."

"If Lefty ain't already dead," Hank added, "then you can bet he's facing a rope."

"Ain't nobody ever going to hang me," Ford said. "And I ain't going back to prison, either."

In the moments they were running from the marshals' attack, Hank had felt a dampness on the inside of his leg, figuring it was simply the result of blood dripping from the bullet's crease on his side.

Now that he had sufficient time to evaluate his situation, Hank learned the moisture on his leg hadn't been blood.

It was water.

During the shootout with the marshals, an errant shot had pierced Hank's canteen close to the bottom, leaving it with no more than a couple swallows of water remaining. Metcalf's once full canteen had been spilling out the precious, life-giving liquid on his leg and boots.

Metcalf knew that Bill's horse had been frightened by the shooting and galloped away to parts unknown, the animal taking one canteen with him. That situation had required Ford to commandeer Lefty's horse. When they left Pitts behind, Ford also returned his canteen and gear back to Lefty at the line shack. leaving Ford's new mount without a canteen.

"Sid, how much water do you have left," Metcalf asked.

Russell nodded his head and lifted the canteen to swirl the remaining contents. There wasn't much water left to slosh around inside.

"Maybe enough to get me through the day," he replied.

"I was afraid of that," Hank said. "If those damn lawmen don't kill us first, our shortage of water might just do it for them." Metcalf then turned his attention to Ford. "How's your shoulder, Bill?"

Ford let go of the reins and reached back inside his coat. He pulled back his hand and studied the amount of blood on his palm. "Looks like it's almost quit bleeding, Hank. The bullet must have went clean through. Reckon I'll live."

Russell checked his back trail, but he saw no signs of the lawmen yet. "I'm thinking those lawmen will be coming for us soon. We'd better be going."

"Well, I've been doing some thinking of my own," Ford said, "about that there woman who put the hurting on Lefty Pitts. It seems we owe her for what she done to him." His remaining green teeth formed an evil smile. "Let me have just one hour alone with her and that little darlin' won't do no more harm to anyone else. But she'll be sure to put a smile on my face before I'm done with her."

"She isn't too far ahead of us," Russell said, pointing down at the ground. "Those are her tracks. Maybe she needs water, too."

"You can forget all that talk for now," Hank said, as he continued riding. "A woman's the last thing we need right now, boys. We've got those lawmen on our trail and we're needing water, bad. The closest water I know about from here is Webster Springs."

"Why don't we just wait along the trail," Ford said, "and pick them off as they ride past." He spat a green stream of tobacco juice into the dust. "It would be easy."

"It might be easy, any other time," Hank replied, "but not now. There's only two things keeping us from holing up and waiting to ambush them. One of them is our shortage of water. The other one is the marshal."

"You mean Miles Olsen?" Russell said. "I ain't scared of him."

"Olsen doesn't scare me either," Metcalf said. "But Olsen isn't alone. That other man is Braxton Poole, the U.S. Marshal. I recognized him, back there at the line shack. Only a fool would take Poole lightly."

"What are we going to do about them, Hank?" Russell asked.

"Nothing for now. We're going to try to stay ahead of the marshals until we can find water. It ought to be easy, with them slowed down by a lumbering pack horse. As far as I know the nearest water from here is at Webster Springs." Metcalf flashed a knowing smile. "If I'm not mistaken, we won't be the only ones needing water."

Sid Russell guessed the rest of it. "And once we get to water, we wait for the marshals there. Then we kill them, don't we, boss."

Metcalf nodded. "That's the way I figure it."

Bill Ford was strangely silent for a time, a quality unlike the burly outlaw, who always had something to say about every situation. His mind had already returned to the woman from the line shack and the carnal possibilities she offered.

"Yeah," Ford added, "it looks like the woman is searching for water too. Maybe this will work out good for all of us. Only thing I like more than killing a lawman is climbing in the saddle with a fine woman."

"Well, don't be like Lefty," Russell said, with a pleased chuckle. "Make damn sure you check your cinch first."

Chapter Fifteen

Webster Springs took its name from legendary figure, Jeremiah Webster, a trapper and mountain man, who became one of the first whites to explore and map out this region of the West.

Webster occasionally teamed with other famous explorers of his era, men such as Jim Beckwourth, who opened up the region for emigrants who would later follow the crucial trails they discovered and established.

There were numerous reasons to believe that Webster's body was buried somewhere nearby, an area which he truly loved and made his home.

According to legend, after his death, Webster was hidden and interred by the natives, who were directed by the Indian woman he chose for his bride. Her tribe held the mountain man in high regard and embraced him as one of their own, but never revealed the location of Webster's remains.

The spring which bore his name was fed by waters that continually flowed down from out of the nearby mountain, forming a pool of water no less than fifteen feet deep. The continual runoff kept the water from becoming stagnant. The runoff also formed the headwaters for a mighty river.

Webster Springs remained fresh and sweet through any kind of weather.

The native Indians knew of its presence for at least a century. The whites only learned of the water's existence in the past twenty years, but few had dared to venture into the area because it was often the realm of hostile Apaches.

Like many of the most reliable sources of water in the West, this rare and flowing oasis was owned by no one, but soon would be claimed by many. Once it became more widely acknowledged, Webster Springs was certain to become the target of railroad executives, land speculators, and cattle barons; anyone with the money to invest, wealthy and influential people, looking for a continuous and dependable source of water in an often dry and barren land.

All these men were cognizant of one truth: in this part of the country, abundant water was indeed wealth. They all figured to make it theirs, just as soon as Victorio and his band of renegade Apaches were safely ensconced back on the reservation.

Their time and their plans would eventually come to fruition, but on this day, Webster Springs was kept under the watchful eye of an Apache, who only wished to steal the horse of Crenshaw's wife.

Kicking Deer decided that the winning of Blue Dove would have to wait.

As much as he desired to take the maiden into his own lodge, he also coveted the respect of his fellow warriors even more. Kicking Deer knew that coming back with an extra horse would make him a big warrior among his people. He figured the stealing of another horse was worth the risk of losing Blue Dove.

But there had been one risk he was not willing to take.

That one would have to come later.

While trailing Crenshaw's woman and her horse, Kicking Deer became aware that she wasn't the only one being tracked. A pair of lawmen were trailing him as well.

At first, Kicking Deer sensed it more than he could see it, but he eventually deceived them with his tracks and glimpsed the one named Poole. The man was known among his people as a strong warrior. *Maybe*, Kicking Deer thought, *I will test him sometime soon*. For now, he decided a fight with Poole and the other lawman might alert the woman to the danger she faced.

Kicking Deer was certain the two men would eventually meet.

He spent the night here, sleeping under the stars, dreaming of Blue Dove. It was a long time to wait, because the Whites traveled much slower than the Apache. He figured the woman should arrive later that day.

Kicking Deer waited off in the distance, keeping the spring in clear view. He lurked almost a half mile ahead of where the thirsty white woman must come to get water. His was a good spot, with excellent cover for a warrior who could remain still.

It was a quality he long had mastered. Kicking Deer excelled at remaining motionless for hours.

He had only to wait.

The prey would soon come to the hunter.

As Kicking Deer stared off into the distance, however, he could see the dust of the woman's horse, the fine horse he wanted, ridden by Crenshaw's woman.

That was not all he could see.

Shielding his eyes against the blinding of the sun, Kicking Deer also spied the cloudy dust from several horses, less than a mile behind the woman.

The Apache smiled.

Perhaps he would return for Blue Dove with many horses.

* * *

A brutal and relentless golden sun beat down upon the horse and the pair of parched and weary riders.

Sarah's horse plodded on, often with little direction.

The endless hours without a drink of water to quench her thirst had inflicted a terrible toll on Sarah Crenshaw. Her son was thirsty too, but like any good mother, Sarah had given the last of their liquid supply to him.

Because of her sacrifice, Sam was suffering far less of the ill effects from going too long without water, but her son was still tired and exhausted from the endless heat. Still, Sarah also realized that even this one bright spot would never amount to much if they didn't find some water soon.

Her unselfishness, however, was not without its own set of hardships. The downside to giving away her meager ration of water was that the woman who needed to lead the two of them to safety was now laboring to think clearly.

As they rode, Sarah leaned her head over Sam's tiny body, hoping that she could provide some shade to him and shield Sam from the unyielding rays of the sun.

Sarah struggled to remain in the saddle. Despite her dizziness and confusion, Sarah believed she was on the right path to make Webster Springs. The woman was also driven to push forward and give no quarter to the weakness inside of her, because of the needs of her son.

Had it only been her life in danger, Sarah knew she would have already given up and yielded to her weakest impulses. Perhaps she would have already been dead.

Looking up at the heavens in false expectations that a rain cloud might have suddenly appeared, Sarah swore softly at her own selfishness and reckless choices. Had she chosen to remain at home and endure just one more day of Ben's drunken abuse, then Sam's life wouldn't now be in danger. Yet almost as soon as the thought passed through her mind, Sarah remembered that Ben hadn't only raised his hand to his wife; he had also struck his own son, Sarah's child.

Despite their circumstances, Sarah dismissed her doubts and knew she made the right decision, the only choice for Sam's ultimate protection.

In that one moment, Sarah mysteriously discovered an inner strength and resolve unlike anything she had ever known. It fueled and refreshed her spirit in ways that mere water never could.

Sarah gained some steel in her spine and a determination that she would survive this hardship and carve out a better life for her and her son.

The two of them would indeed live.

She was sure of it.

While crossing a dry creek bed, a place where waters would run thirty foot deep and fifty feet wide during a summer storm, Sarah drew rein. Climbing down from her horse, she grabbed hold of the cinch to regain her balance.

Once Sarah felt the wave of dizziness and nausea had passed, she began to search the ground. After a moment, she found exactly what she had been seeking. Sarah picked up a small, smooth stone and placed it between her dry and cracking lips, a technique her father once told her would help to produce some moisture in one's mouth.

Sarah was skeptical of this ancient survival trick, but at least the prospects of relief offered some small measure of hope to her situation.

Hope, it was a quality in short supply now.

Much like the water they needed.

Chapter Sixteen

The lack of water hadn't only inflicted a dreadful toll upon the woman and her son; it also led to misery and endless conflict between the three outlaws. Lately, as their thirst for water grew more desperate, their hostilities increased, approaching the point of violence.

"None of this would have happened," Bill Ford said, "if Lefty Pitts hadn't lost my horse."

For the last ten miles, Ford had done nothing but grumble about their situation, gripes that were constantly reminding the others of their need for water. Sid Russell was growing weary of his complaints and almost longed for the return of Ford's long-winded tales about what depravities he planned for the woman.

"I'm telling you, Bill, I've heard just about enough about your horse. Pitts was a good friend of mine for a heap of years. And the way I figure it, you were the one who let your own horse get away, not Lefty. So, why don't you quit running your jaws?"

At this latest remark, Ford drew rein and stopped. He glared over at Russell before speaking. "If you think you're man enough to shut my mouth, why don't you go ahead and pull that gun of yours and try it?"

All of these disputes were starting to annoy Hank Metcalf, who was focused solely on finding water and getting the two lawmen off their trail. Although he momentarily left Poole and Olsen somewhere behind them, Hank was familiar with the reputation of Braxton Poole.

Based on that knowledge, Hank guessed that their pursuit was only beginning and the outlaws' need for running was far from over.

"If you two men want a fight so bad," Hank said, "why don't you just ride on back there and square off against Marshal Braxton Poole?

I'm sure the man will give you all the fight you ever want." Metcalf reined his horse around until it was directly facing the mount that Ford was riding. "And there's one other thing, Bill."

"What's that?"

"I'm the one who invited Lefty Pitts to trail along with us. I'm the one running this outfit. And it's me who makes the decisions about who leaves this gang and when. It's not you," Hank said, as he smiled without humor. "You're welcome to challenge those decisions whenever you've had enough of living. You can even take your gear—or Lefty's gear—and pull out anytime you want." Hank pulled his coat away from the butt of his six-gun. "But if you dare to second guess me one more time, you damn well better have a gun in your hand when you do it. Is that clear?"

Bill said nothing.

Metcalf refused to let the matter drop without a response. "I said, do you understand me?"

"Yes, boss."

Bill Ford wasn't a man accustomed to being talked to in this manner. In fact, he killed the last two men who dared to do it. Now it happened with both Sid and Hank. The verbal slights were too much for him to stomach. Even as he conceded this one time to Metcalf, Ford made up his mind that he would eventually have to kill the man who led them. He also realized that day would bring him great pleasure.

"Now that we're done with this bickering," Hank said, "let's set our minds on getting to Webster Springs."

* * *

Despite her earlier confidence, Sarah now doubted herself that she actually knew the water's true location. Perhaps she was wrong about Webster Springs. As her horse continued plodding along, the woman's mind was a dark and bloody battlefield, with the forces of fear winning all the high ground.

As much as she wanted to give up, Sarah realized that her failure would ultimately result in the death of her child. Although Sarah didn't believe her life was all that important to anybody still living, it was certain Sam would lose his life unless she prevailed in this quest.

With eyes full of love and wonder, thankful for this precious life which was placed in her custody, Sarah glanced down at Sam, astride the horse, riding between her knees as he leaned his head against her chest. It was the same child that grew inside her womb, sprang from her own loins, and nourished himself from her own bosom.

She loved him with her entire soul.

But it broke her heart, thinking she may have indeed failed him.

Finally, weakness got the better of her and the woman decided it was time to tell her son the bitter truth. Sarah could no longer live with the facts she'd been concealing from him. She also believed that, even if she perished out here, perhaps her child would find water and survive. It was her only remaining source of hope. There was also a chance that the lawmen, those ones she believed would soon come to arrest her, might discover Sam before it was too late to save him.

Sarah knew it was time to tell Sam the sad truth about their situation.

"Sam, she said, "I have to talk to you."

"Yes, Mama," he replied, a trustful set of eyes staring up into ones filled with worried tears.

"I need to tell you . . ."

Sarah never finished her sentence, as her eyes lifted to glimpse the unexpected, but welcoming sight of Webster Springs, the one place she was so desperately seeking.

Sarah was right in her recollection; she *had* remembered its location.

Sarah breathed a sigh of relief that her impetuous actions at home hadn't brought a curse upon her own son. Moreover, her defense of Sam wasn't only responsible for helping him to escape from the dangers of a brutal homelife; the woman, whose womb gave him life, now saved his life out here as well.

The weary and frightened woman didn't know whether she should cry or laugh, but at that very moment, she found herself doing both. Sarah raised her eyes skyward as her lips mouthed a silent prayer of thanks to the guardian of fools.

"What is it, Mama? Why are you crying."

"I'm happy."

"Then why are you crying?"

She wiped her eyes and hugged his tiny body even closer to her chest. "We've found it," Sarah said. "We found water. We found Webster Springs."

Sarah put the strong and tired horse into a trot until her mount came to the edge of the water and sunk its lips into the liquid and began to drink its fill.

"Can I have a drink?"

"You bet you can."

Her dirty countenance was beaming, as happy tears rolled down her cheeks, tracing lines upon her face as the tears washed away the dust, before dropping from her jaws into the dirt.

Upon seeing the tear-streaked face of his mother, the child began to laugh and point at her. "You look like a painted Indian, Mama."

Sarah climbed down from her horse and scooped up a handful of water, taking just a quick taste to make sure it wasn't brackish or undrinkable for her son. Then she washed her hands in the spring and filled both hands with water, which she offered to a thirsty Sam, who tried to lap up every drop.

Like any young boy around water, Sam wasn't simply satisfied with drinking from the spring. He waded out into the water, clear up to his knees and played. Instead of scolding the boy, Sarah grabbed the canteen from their horse and joined him.

Sarah filled their canteen, sharing the sweet, fresh water from it between her and her son. The woman was also aware that she shouldn't let them drink too much of this precious liquid at first, allowing their parched and exhausted bodies to grow accustomed to the sudden change in conditions.

Knowing how critically important this water was to their survival, once they both drank their fill, the woman carefully replaced the lid, and hung the canteen around her neck.

Her thirst finally quenched, Sarah began to wash away the dust from her face, arms, and neck. The feel of the cool water on her body was delightful and refreshing. It not only chased away her thirst, but it helped to revitalize her spirit.

Once satisfied that she had done all she could to improve her appearance, Sarah began to splash handfuls of water on Sam. He did the same to her as well, the two of them splashing and playing at the spring, behaving like a pair of young children.

After leaving the water, Sarah made sure they were fed and laid out a blanket upon which they could sleep. Fearful that she would sleep so soundly the horse would wander off, Sarah wrapped the ends of the reins around her arm and tied them.

The horse lowered his head and began to crop grass as the two weary travelers dozed in the sunlight.

Lurking on a hill not too far away from the water, Kicking Deer watched as the two of them spread out a blanket to rest. He waited until the woman and the son grew still and appeared to be slumbering.

Confident they were asleep, the Apache pulled his knife and started inching toward the unsuspecting mother and her young child.

Chapter Seventeen

When outlaws are fleeing from the blasts of hostile gunfire, the last thing on their minds is the need to conceal their trail. It was for that reason, Marshals Poole and Olsen followed their tracks with little effort. Even while leading the pack horse, they were still making good time. The two lawmen also had the advantage of knowing where the outlaws were most likely headed.

Like the pair of determined marshals, the outlaws needed to find water. Poole suspected that the woman and her child were also facing those same hardships while riding through this barren and desolate land.

Ever since they first came upon the tracks of Sarah Crenshaw, Marshal Poole became impressed with her courage and tenacity. Although he was somewhat acquainted with Sarah before she married Ben Crenshaw, and he and the woman had a few occasions to speak in town afterwards, this was a side of the woman he had never seen.

Poole's time as a lawman made him witness to many atrocities and unspeakable acts of random violence . Those experiences resulted in him growing skeptical about life and people in general. Very few things impressed him now. People rarely did.

Yet at this very moment, Braxton Poole admired this extraordinary woman's courage and her dogged will to survive. He also marveled at her singular desire to save her son. Sarah was indeed strong and resourceful. The woman was much too good a person to die at the hands of these bandits. It was for those reasons that Poole had no desire to fail this woman in return.

Theirs was to be a harrowing journey, one that would take all seven of these thirsty travelers—woman, men, and child—to the same destination . . .

The waters of Webster Springs.

Poole was also conscious of the fact that this situation was not without its own disadvantages as well. The outlaws knew their pursuers would also need to find water, although the marshals started out better supplied, resulting in their situation being less desperate. There was no way for the marshals to prevent Metcalf and his gang from reaching the water first, leaving the outlaws rested and refreshed, along with being armed and ready.

No doubt the three men in Metcalf's gang would be waiting at the springs to kill the pair of tired lawmen.

Although he made no effort to speak of it to Miles, Poole's greatest fear remained the knowledge that the woman would have to face these deadly and dangerous men alone, including the evil Bill Ford.

* * *

Growing up on a small farm in western Kentucky, raising tobacco and cotton, a young Hank Metcalf longed to forever get away from the plow and explore the excitement of just about anywhere else.

After the firing on Fort Sumter, Hank enlisted in the Confederate army. Hank served with honor for over two years, impressing his fellow soldiers along with his superiors due to his remarkable courage under fire. Rumor had it that the bold, young private was even considered for a battlefield promotion, talk that was soon quashed with the unexpected news of his desertion.

Like a ship without a rudder, Metcalf drifted around for a while after the war, eventually moving to Texas. From there, he hired on as a drover, taking part in several cattle drives headed to Kansas. On one of those drives, after pinning the herd at the railhead three month later, Metcalf walked a little taller with the feel of those hard-earned wages filling his once-empty pockets.

The unhealthy combination of youthful pride and liquor led to a heated dispute with the madam at one of the town's brothels. When the madam ordered her hired muscle to forcibly remove Hank from the establishment, Metcalf gunned him down right there on their lobby's fine, imported carpet.

It was the killing at the brothel that started Hank Metcalf on the run from the law, leading him to commit other crimes, a condition which soon revealed that larceny and murder clearly suited his tastes.

Since those early days, Hank teamed up with a number of outlaws, additional pairings that rarely lasted long and often divided with gunplay. But in those times after General Lee's surrender at Appomattox, there was no shortage of young men out there, veterans of the war, looking to make some easy money.

Mysteriously, Hank Metcalf lived to grow much older than others who plied his trade. Even the Pinkertons failed to catch him. Marshal Braxton Poole was the only lawman who ever brought Metcalf to justice.

Perhaps it was his endless desire to roam, never staying in one place too long, that made him difficult to catch. No doubt Metcalf's persistent demands for obedience and his inability to remain with one specific group of outlaws also factored in his longevity.

The years that followed did absolutely nothing to mellow Hank Metcalf; they made him worse. Metcalf insisted on giving orders and having them followed, a lesson that Bill Ford was just starting to learn.

Even these many hours later, Ford was still rankled about Hank's scolding.

Although he was a fair hand with a shooting iron, Bill knew he was no match for Hank's skills. Despite that knowledge, he believed Metcalf was careless at times and the man might be easily gunned down if taken by surprise.

But Ford was not a fool.

As long as they were being chased by the two marshals, Bill knew he might have need of Hank's gun to even up the numbers. Yet when that need no longer existed, then he figured that Metcalf would indeed be expendable. Once they found water and dealt with the lawmen, then Bill figured he would look for an opportunity to kill Hank and then become the leader for a change.

Even greater than his current desire for water and revenge, Ford's thoughts were now dominated by his lust for the woman, a woman scarcely ahead of them.

"I remember you saying you've been this way before," Hank said, while drawing rein and mopping his brow on his shirt sleeve. "How close do you think we are, Sid?"

Russell struggled to stay in the saddle, his mind increasingly addled and irritated by endless questions about the spring's location.

"It can't be more than two or three miles at the most, boss."

"It better be."

"If you know a quicker route, you're welcome to find it your own self," Russell replied. Yet even in his weakened and weary state, Sid feared to speak to Metcalf in a flippant manner. "Don't pay me no mind, boss. I'm just a mite done in."

Coming from Russell, a man he had no reason to fear, Hank merely laughed it off. "It's nothing, Sid. We're all feeling the same way."

Russell breathed a little easier as he studied the trail and resumed riding. The other two outlaws started their horses along behind him.

Their horses slogged on the trail for another miserable hour.

Russell said, "I'd kill for a drink right now."

"Before this is all over, you might have to," Ford observed. "Do you still have that bottle of rotgut in your saddlebags?"

"Yeah, I do, but liquor won't help your thirst none," he replied, reaching into his saddlebags. He handed over the bottle to Bill.

Ford pulled the stopper and took a long pull. "Maybe not, but it will make me forget about how thirsty I am." He held up the bottle to Hank. "You want a taste?"

Russell wasn't the only one who realized that liquor wasn't a viable substitute for water. Hank knew it would only make his problems worse. "No, Bill, you go ahead," Hank said. "It's all yours."

Ford just laughed and took another drink.

Watching the man compound his difficulties by pouring liquor on them, Metcalf found himself wishing that Ford was the one who was killed, instead of Lefty Pitts. Hank also noticed the way Bill looked at him when he thought nobody was watching. He'd seen that sort of behavior before, with other gangs, with other men. It always led to gunplay and somebody dead. Metcalf was under no illusions that this time would be any different from the other times.

If he wanted to maintain control of the gang, Hank would eventually have to draw his gun on Bill Ford and one of them would likely die.

As their horses continued down the trail, Hank watched Sid Russell fighting to remain in his saddle. At times, he was scarcely conscious. He knew they were going to be dead if they didn't find water before nightfall. He couldn't believe that Ford's drinking hadn't done him in by now. All Hank could figure is that Bill was solely driven only by his carnal urges for the woman.

Afraid that any sign of weakness on his part would leave him vulnerable to a challenge in his leadership of the gang, Hank strove to keep his wits about him. Increasingly, the lack of water made it difficult for him to focus.

Hank swung down from his saddle and stumbled a little the moment his boot hit the ground. He stopped himself from falling by grabbing the cinch on his mount. Once convinced he could finally stand on his own, Hank let go of the animal and attempted to regain his composure.

"We'd better walk a while and give these horses a break."

The two other outlaws looked disgusted as they relented and climbed down from their saddles.

Upon stepping down, Ford fell into the dust, the liquor now having its full effect on the man. He laughed stupidly at his state.

For just a moment Hank considered killing Ford before he ever had the chance to regain his footing. If not for the risk of alerting the lawmen to their presence, he might have acted on the notion. Metcalf was not a fool, either. Although Ford would be a formidable enemy, Hank also knew that his gun would be needed during any kind of a shooting scrape with Marshal Poole . . .

If they lived long enough.

Chapter Eighteen

Miles Olsen climbed down from his saddle to study the trail. He only spent a couple of moments before returning to his horse. When Olsen forked his saddle again, he didn't even get the chance to explain what he learned.

"Don't bother telling me, Miles. I can see it without getting down. Sarah and those bandits are all headed towards the same place. This trail will be coming to an end at Webster Springs."

He took a final sip of the water and handed the canteen to his friend for their last drink. Olsen drained the remaining liquid out of the canteen, closed the lid, and handed it back to Poole, who hung it over his saddle horn.

"Yeah, Braxton, I'm sure it looks bad to you," Olsen replied, noting the worry in his friend's eyes, "but we'll get her back."

"How can you say that for sure?"

"We already know Mrs. Crenshaw is a fighter. Maybe she and the boy will get through this unharmed."

"I appreciate you trying to make me feel better about this, Miles, especially after me being so hard on you lately."

"I've already forgotten about that."

"No, Miles, please, I need to finish this. I shouldn't have spoken that way to you, ever. This isn't an excuse; it's just an explanation. These men are nothing more than animals, killing and maiming innocent people for their own pleasure. It's doubtful that I'll get out of this alive.

"If for some reason I don't make it, but Sarah and little Sam survive," Poole continued, "please make sure to sell all my possessions and direct that money to them. Promise me, Miles."

He offered his hand to Poole, who shook his in return. "You can count on me, Braxton. I'll see they're cared for. Now there's something else I need to say."

"What is it?"

"From what we saw back there at the Crenshaw ranch and at the line shack, we already know Mrs. Crenshaw is a tough lady, obviously something of a scrapper," Olsen said. "And if I'm guessing, I think both of those incidents happened because she was protecting her son. Along with being a tough lady, the fact that she and the boy are still alive and somewhere ahead of us tells me that she is a smart one too.

"What kind of a woman is capable of living through all of this, finding water, while also saving her boy in the process?" Miles continued. "If you ask me, she sounds like a woman to ride the river with. So, if you had money to bet on only one person in this life, Braxton, you'd be wise to stake your whole fortune on her. I'm telling you; Mrs. Crenshaw will make it."

"I hope you're right."

"I'm sure I am. I've just got myself a hunch about that one."

They rode without talking for about a mile. Miles could see that Poole's head was clearly somewhere else. Despite their thirst, the marshal guessed his friend wasn't doing any deep contemplation about water.

Never a talkative soul, Braxton Poole was always a man of action. He had already spoken more on this trip than Olsen ever experienced. His behavior amounted to a change in habit that was odd for the U.S. Marshal. Apparently, Poole wasn't done talking.

It was Poole who finally broke the strange silence.

"Tell me, Miles, who am I? I mean, what kind of man spends his time thinking about building a future with a woman who scarcely knows him?"

Olsen sighed and laughed. "A lonely one, I'd imagine."

At nearly the same time—and without talking about it first—both men drew rein and started checking their guns.

"You think they'll be waiting for us, Braxton?"

"Yes, I do."

"I thought the same thing."

"We may have to wait until nightfall to make our play," Poole said. "It could be our only chance of rescuing Sarah and the boy."

"If it ups the odds of us getting out alive, you've got my vote."

Poole smiled and winked. "You didn't hear me, Miles. I never said anything about us getting out alive."

* * *

Bone-dry and dog-tired, the three outlaws led their horses for almost half a mile before remounting. Twice, they needed to stop long enough for Bill to retch up the contents of his stomach. The first time, it all spilled upon the dusty ground. The second time, Ford only experienced dry heaves.

"I told you that liquor wasn't a good idea, Bill," Russell said.

"Mind your own damn business," Ford replied. "If I wasn't so sick, I'd beat you like a two-bit whore."

For the first time since they started riding with Metcalf, Russell believed he finally had the upper hand with the burly outlaw. "I'm right here, big man."

Angered by Russell's statement, and slumped over from his pain, Ford removed the hand that was holding his churning insides and stood as tall as his six-foot frame would allow. "If we ever make it to water, I'm going to kill you, Sid. You can count on it."

"If you two ladies feel good enough to fight, then you feel good enough to walk," Hank said. "Let's get moving. We need that water. You take the lead, Sid."

Despite his weakness and desire to quit, Metcalf pushed onward, driven by his desire to remain free and his fear of a hangman's rope. After twenty minutes of walking, Bill Ford stumbled and fell into the dirt. The two outlaws helped Bill to his feet.

Ten minutes later, Sid Russell collapsed as well.

With each one of them nearly at the point of going no farther, it was Metcalf's idea that their best chance of survival was to climb back in their saddles. Hank knew they were dead men, unless the nearly spent horses could carry them to safety.

Almost to the point of exhaustion, Ford looked for anything to take his mind off their condition. Russell's throat was so dry, he couldn't even spit. Finally, he decided that talking might distract his mind from their need for water.

"You act like there's some history between you and this Poole fellow, boss. What can you tell us about him?"

"I'm too wore out to talk about it now, but I will make you a promise, Sid."

"A promise? What do you mean?"

A smile formed on Hank's dry and cracked lips. "If you can find Webster Springs, I'll tell you all about it, over a drink of cool, sweet water."

Russell nodded and went back to studying the horizon for familiar markings. Despite his muddled state of mind, Sid remained confident in the ultimate success of their path.

His voice hoarse and barely above a whisper, Ford observed, "I don't know why you keep listening to this man, Hank. He's going to get us all killed."

"What about you, Bill? You have any better ideas?" Metcalf asked, his palm inching near the butt of his gun. The outlaw's patience was running in short supply, nearly as empty as their dry canteens. "Maybe you can lead us to water. Maybe you'd like to show us how it's done, then. Go ahead, show us, damn you. Show us."

Russell could see the growing doubts in the eyes of the two of them. Although Sid cared nothing about winning Ford's respect, the same couldn't be said for his thoughts about Metcalf, a man he idolized.

"We're getting close, boss. I know it."

"Okay then, it's decided," Hank said. "We're counting on you, Sid. Now, let's ride."

Then the three parched outlaws started their horses on down the trail, riding to what they all hoped was a source of life-giving water.

* * *

With his razor-sharp blade glinting in the sunlight, Kicking Deer was only about fifty feet away from his two unsuspecting victims when he first saw the dust of the approaching riders. As much as he wanted to kill the woman and take her fine horse, the Apache didn't think it wise to be seen by the others.

Perhaps if he waited, there would be a chance for his blade to not only kill the woman; maybe it might also taste the blood of several more of the White devils. The Indian brave believed he could kill some more of them and take all their horses back to his camp.

Kicking Deer sprinted back behind cover only mere seconds before the young boy lifted his head.

"Mama, I hear something," Sam said. It was then he saw the dust of approaching horses somewhere off in the distance. "Look over there."

Sarah lifted her head at the sound of his stirring. "I see them too."

Conscious of her current state of undress, she scrambled to put her now-dry dress back on over her bloomers. Knowing nothing of the riders who were headed their way, and as an added measure of safety, Sarah also buckled the gun belt around her hips and cradled the rifle in her arms.

Continuing to look into the distance and shielding her eyes against the sun, Sarah Crenshaw could see there were three riders coming their way. The woman and her son moved over next to the horse as they approached.

Chapter Nineteen

Leading the trio of three outlaws, Sid Russell swayed from side to side in the saddle. Once, his head slumped so far forward that he was stirred back to consciousness by bumping his forehead on the saddle horn.

The other two outlaws were in no better shape than Sid was. All of them were barely holding on, less than a couple of hours away from a dry and bitter death.

As they topped a rise, Sid stopped his horse and stared off into the distance. Rubbing his dry eyes and struggling to focus them, Russell feared his brain was playing evil tricks on him.

Hank caught up with his mount and reined in alongside him. "What are you stopping for, Sid? What's there?"

Russell pointed off into the distance. "If my eyes aren't deceiving me, isn't that a woman and a boy out there, standing next to a horse?"

Hank stared off in the direction that Sid's finger was pointing. He said nothing for a time, as if he was in some kind of a trance. Then Hank broke into a big smile. "You're damned right it is, boy. Yeah, Sid, it's a woman all right. But look over to her right. That there's water."

Sid reached over and slapped Metcalf on the back, an action he would have never even considered under normal circumstances. "Damned if we didn't make it, Hank. That's Webster Springs."

Upon seeing the water, Hank let loose with a spirited Rebel Yell and the two men spurred their horses into a gallop. Their mounts raced for the pool of fresh water, leaving the other outlaw several hundred yards behind them.

Ford, scarcely conscious, merely sat on his horse, bewildered. After a couple of moments, Bill came to the realization that his friends found water. Knowing he must follow them to water, Ford leaned forward in the saddle, before toppling off his horse onto the cracked and broken ground.

Still cradling the rifle across her arms, Sarah Crenshaw and her son stood off to the side as the two outlaws raced up to the water's edge. Neither of them made any effort to speak, or in any way acknowledge her, and she was left wondering if the two riders even noted their presence.

Sarah also couldn't understand why they made no effort, or seemed to be in no hurry whatsoever, to help their weary friend, leaving him simply to lie out there alone in the dust.

Although she knew nothing about these three strangers, and still had no reason to suspect them of anything larcenous, it still put her instincts on edge. Sarah clearly knew she wasn't particularly wise to the ways of men with each other, but she didn't imagine that was the sort of behavior one would normally expect out of close friends.

Also to be considered was the safety of her son. If for that reason alone, Sarah elected to proceed with caution in her dealings with these three strangers. She also made a decision to locate her daddy's knife and keep it close at hand.

Both the outlaws dismounted in an instant, Hank's boots hitting the ground before the animal came to a complete stop. Metcalf fell to his knees, before plunging his head underneath the surface.

When he emerged from the pool, he threw back his head, as the wet and dripping hair fell upon the back of his neck. Still not satisfied, Hank sunk his lips in the water and let the cool liquid soothe his parched throat.

The two thirsty horses walked to the water's edge, lowered their necks, and gulped deeply, as if to make up for lost time.

Sid Russell scooped up one handful of water after another, drinking them down as quickly as only a parched man could. After several drinks, Sid dipped his hat in the water and placed it back on his head, soaking his hair, clothes, and body in the process. He feverishly drank some more and then stretched out in the grass, sprawled out peacefully next to the water. Closing his eyes to the blistering sun, he rested.

At that moment, Russell didn't care if the marshals came.

For now, he was alive.

"Sid," Hank said, "why don't you go back out there and give Ford a drink."

Normally obedient to Metcalf's orders, Russell made no effort to move from his place of comfort. "Let him be, boss. He'll be along in a few minutes."

Seeing as how he was a stickler about his orders being followed, Sid's insolence would have generally riled Hank, but not today. Metcalf knew that Russell's knowledge of the water's location had saved all their lives, so he was favorably inclined to give the younger outlaw a pass for his behavior.

Metcalf, sadly recognizing that he still needed a third gun whenever the marshals arrived, decided to ride back and help Bill. It was difficult for him to ignore his first impulse, which was to let the man lie out there and die, but he needed Ford.

At least for now he did.

Hank reluctantly forked his saddle and rode back out to where the bandit had fallen. He climbed down from horseback and stooped down next to the body of the unconscious man.

Exhibiting a measure of strength that seemed unlikely for a man of his size, Hank somehow lifted the burly outlaw to his shoulders. From there, he tossed him face first over Ford's saddlehorse.

Once back on horseback, Hank caught up Ford's horse by the reins, with the outlaw sprawled over the saddle the way one would do with a dead body. From there, he proceeded to lead the animal back to the springs, leaving Ford's horse parallel to the water's edge.

For a moment Hank just sat there, figuring the belligerent riding partner would snap out of his unconscious state now that he was this close to fresh, cool water, especially since the horse began to drink. Seeing that his hunch was wrong, Metcalf uttered a profanity underneath his breath and spurred his horse alongside Bill's.

What Metcalf did next caused Sarah to gasp with surprise, for Hank reached over, grabbed the heel of Ford's boot and lifted, dumping the fallen outlaw head first into the cool and pleasant waters of Webster Springs.

As Metcalf watched the outlaw gasp, spit, and curse, before coming to his feet, he thought about how much he regretted fouling those sweet waters with the stale, unsavory body of Bill Ford.

From the ground beside them, Russell never moved except to lazily open one eye and softly state, "Hey, boss, ain't you glad you had brains enough to get a clean drink from out of there first?" Once making the statement, Russell reclosed his eye and drifted back to sleep.

With his thirst now satisfied and his partners safely to the water, Hank walked over to introduce himself to the woman.

As he approached her, Hank saw Sarah was a handsome woman, still rather young, but lovely in both face and form. A ring was on her finger, so she obviously was married to someone—or had been. He was puzzled, however, about the few blood stains that marked her dress.

His quick appraisal also told him the woman was wary of them, or perhaps of any stranger, because of the way she kept her rifle at the ready. Hank smiled. *Smart woman, that one.*

"My name's Hank Metcalf," he said, gently touching the brim of his hat.

Sarah did her best to reveal nothing, but Hank thought he detected a glint of recognition in her eyes as he spoke the name. He also thought she may have taken a little firmer grip on the weapon she was holding.

"The fellow napping is Sid Russell. Bill Ford is the one out in the water drowning. He'll probably be fine in a few minutes. Please excuse Bill's foul mouth, if you will. We're drifting cowhands, looking for work. And you are?"

"I am Sarah Crenshaw, the wife of a rancher. This is my son Sam."

"Pleased to meet you, ma'am. Same with you, son," he said, reaching out to shake the boy's hand. "You've got a good, strong handshake, Sam. That's good. I hope you don't mind us sharing your water, ma'am."

"Not at all, Mr. Metcalf. It's not really ours. It would appear that we were just the first arrivals," Sarah replied, smiling as she said it.

Her kind and genuine smile made the woman's face even more lovely than he first realized, a quality that would definitely add fuel to Ford's most depraved urges. Perhaps her presence would be something to keep the burly outlaw awake and entertained until the marshals attacked them. Hank also couldn't escape the idea that the lovely Mrs. Crenshaw reminded him of someone, but he could not identify who that someone was.

Hank genuinely returned the woman's smile. "I couldn't help but notice, that's a nice horse you have. Does your husband raise them?"

Sam started to say something, leaving Sarah fearful that he would spill the beans about her husband's state. She removed one hand from the rifle and pinched the child's ear, something she often did to silence Sam when he was talking too much.

Her sudden action was not lost on the outlaw, for it was something his own mother often did to him when he was young.

"Sam," she said, not wanting the boy to hear her lie, "why don't you go see to the horse. You stay close now, you hear?"

"Yes, Mama," he replied. "I will."

Hank watched him go. "That, there, is an obedient kid, Mrs. Crenshaw. You should be proud."

"I am, Mr. Metcalf, very proud."

"Excuse me for my short memory. We were talking about horses, weren't we?"

"Yes, Mr. Metcalf, we have a few horses, but nothing to sell right now. Ben, my husband, is supposed to be meeting us here, at almost any time," she said, lying. Sarah looked at the sky, as if to check the position of the sun. I can't imagine what's keeping him. Oh, never mind. I'm sure he'll be along before nightfall."

Not believing a word of the woman's story, Hank nodded. "I'm sure he will, ma'am. Now if you will excuse me, like your son, I have to see to *our* horses."

Metcalf suspected the woman was traveling alone and told him those lies to protect her own safety. Perhaps Mrs. Crenshaw was afraid she would be molested in some fashion by these strangers, a fear that had some real basis in fact with a man like Bill Ford in her camp. Still, he doubted that the Crenshaw woman was familiar with Ford's name and reputation.

The same could not be said about his own name. She had recognized the surname. Hank was sure of it. At the same time, he also knew there was little harm to come from that knowledge. The law already knew who he was, where they were, and Marshal Poole would soon be coming to capture them.

Hank determined that it would still be a good idea to keep his eyes on Mrs. Crenshaw. She might prove to be a problem for them. Then again, Hank also concluded that the woman and her son might come in handy as well.

* * *

As he made his way back to the horses, Metcalf, who generally planned for every eventuality, had no idea he was being examined by another set of eyes.

Off in the distance and thoroughly concealed, Kicking Deer observed the arrival of the three men to the water. The things he saw pleased him. Most of his interest focused on their mounts, all of them good horses that would win Kicking Deer much favor upon returning to his camp.

The Apache warrior instantly resolved to make those horses his own, either through theft or by killing their riders, two options of which he held no preference.

Kicking Deer speculated that these three white men were the ones that Poole and his friend were hunting. Like the pair of lawmen, the Indian had studied their tracks as well and their intentions were clear to him. Theirs was a confrontation Kicking Deer greatly wished to avoid.

He knew Poole would be a formidable opponent in battle and Kicking Deer longed to test him. But their eventual struggle for supremacy would have to wait. At this time, he would simply be satisfied with stealing these four horses and winning the hand of Blue Dove.

Nothing else mattered to him at the moment.

Formulating a plan in his mind, Kicking Deer decided that he would wait until the darkness was upon them. That is the time when he would make his move. Once they bedded down for the night, he guessed that only one of them would remain on guard. He also knew that he would have no difficulties in killing the Whites' lone guard.

If it became necessary, Kicking Deer had no compunctions about killing more of these White devils.

There was scarcely any doubt in his mind that he would have their horses before the sun climbed high in the sky again. *Then,* Kicking Deer thought, *I will return to my camp and take Blue Dove into my lodge. She will give me many strong sons, Apache warriors who will free my people from the reservation and defeat the long knives.*

Kicking Deer knew his was a good plan.

With nothing else to be decided, Kicking Deer rolled over on his side and went to sleep, knowing that dreams of Blue Dove would be dancing in his mind.

Chapter Twenty

As the pair of lawmen traversed the dusty landscape, Miles Olsen drew rein suddenly, his actions taking Poole by surprise.

"Why are you stopping, Miles?"

Olsen removed his hat and mopped the sweat from his face with the elbow of his shirt. "We're only about a mile and a half from Webster Springs," he said, returning the hat to cover his bald head. "This is as far as we dare to go on horseback, unless we want to alert Metcalf as to our location."

"That's good thinking. Bad as I hate to do it in this cursed heat, we'll have to go the rest of the way on foot."

Olsen cast a glance skyward. "It looks like there's only about four hours until nightfall. We can rest for now and move out then."

Poole's face was marked with a nervous smile. "About that . . ."

Olsen had seen that look from his friend before. It normally signaled that something unorthodox was fixing to happen, an occurrence that Miles wouldn't much like, probably something that could get them both killed. He grimaced at the thought.

"Out with it now, Braxton. What are you thinking?"

"While we were riding, I was giving this matter some serious thought."

Olsen smiled nervously, but was still curious to learn about the plan hatched in his friend's resourceful mind. "You were, were you?"

Poole climbed down from the saddle before continuing. Olsen did the same, tentatively waiting for the hare-brained scheme that he knew the marshal would soon spell out for him.

"After some careful consideration, I decided that Metcalf would be expecting us to make our move on them after sunset," Poole said, before pausing for a time. He often did that before presenting the worst of the details. "That is why we aren't going to do what Metcalf would assume. Of course, there is some danger involved with this plan, increasing the likelihood that we might be spotted. We're going to take them all by surprise. I figure to hit them when they're least expecting it, before the sun falls."

"I'm obligated to tell you that I hate this plan, Braxton, but it pains me to admit that I agree with your conclusion. If we charge into Metcalf's camp, guns blazing, we won't be able to see our targets. It's hard to tell who we'll hit."

Poole nodded. "I hate it too, Miles, but it may be our best and only chance of keeping Sarah and the boy from being killed. Maybe we can also rid the world of those diseased animals at the same time. So, you're in agreement then?"

"Yes, I am."

"Good," Poole said, "let's gnaw on some of that jerked venison and eat a couple of cold biscuits. Then we'll get ready to roll."

Olsen laughed. "You don't happen to have a spare canteen of water tucked away in your bag of tricks, do you?"

Poole shook his head. "Nope, but I sure wish I did. I reckon we'll get water after we finish our mission." The smile immediately disappeared from the marshal's face and he became as sober as a judge.

"A woman and an innocent little boy need our help, Miles. When the shooting starts, you'd be wise to remember that Sid Russell is a killer, but not our greatest threat. We have to make sure that we kill Metcalf and Ford first. Or we have to die trying."

"You really believe that, don't you?"

"You bet I do. I don't think I would go on living if another woman and child perished again and I was helpless to prevent it."

"I never thought I'd say this, Braxton, but it sounds to me like you're in love with this Crenshaw woman."

"That's crazy talk, coming from you," Poole said, turning suddenly to hide the truth that his face might actually reveal. "Just be sure you focus on what we have to do. You can count on me to do the same."

* * *

A couple of hours after the outlaws first arrived at the water, Hank Metcalf and Sid Russell were going about their business, tired, but healthy as before. The two of them were showing no ill-effects of their brutal, waterless journey.

Sarah didn't think it strange that cowhands might repeatedly check on their horses, but she saw no good explanation for cowhands to be overly concerned about the loading and maintenance of their six-guns and rifles.

Despite their friendly greetings and overtures, Sarah did not trust these men.

In addition, Sarah was also certain that she once heard people in town talking about someone named Metcalf and the crimes carried out by his band of outlaws. The men's preoccupation in keeping their guns in order led her to believe that the rumors about these strangers might indeed be correct.

It was her intention to constantly remain cordial and give the men no hints of her suspicions. She even put her guns away, making it appear that the strangers had won her trust. Meanwhile, Sarah was also formulating plans for her and Sam to ultimately escape, far away from the bandits' reach.

For just a second, Sarah thought about the kind man, Marshal Poole, that she earlier feared would be the one to arrest her. Now, she was wishing the marshal could be here with her and Sam. She was certain Poole would know what to do.

Bill Ford was still suffering the effects of his many hours without water, problems that were compounded by his reckless consumption of alcohol and the loss of blood due to his gunshot wound.

The outlaw spent the last two hours sleeping. Ford only stirred from his slumber on a couple occasions, albeit brief times when he would simply take another drink of water before closing his eyes once again. Even an attractive woman's presence mattered little to him right now.

Seeing that the burly outlaw was still experiencing difficulties from their journey, Hank grew even more concerned about having enough guns to face the pair of capable lawmen. He also concluded that using the woman and her son in a hostage situation might end up being their only means of escape.

It was for this reason—and also for matters of his own ease—that Hank offered the woman the free use of all of their supplies. In return, she prepared a meal and coffee for the assembled crowd, creating a delightful smell that even roused Ford from his seemingly endless slumber.

Now feeling much better and wakened from his slumber, Bill appraised the woman like a man purchasing a horse. His eyes roamed the length of her figure, making her feel dirty and uncomfortable. The soulless look in Ford's eyes left Sarah fearful and shaken. It also made her aware that she must get away soon. Then Bill turned back to his food, wolfing it down greedily.

Russell took his plate and coffee from the woman like it was a chore she was expected to perform, but he made no effort to express any gratitude. The same could not be said for Hank Metcalf, who told her, "Thank you kindly, Mrs. Crenshaw. It's been a long time since a woman prepared a meal for me."

Upon their first meeting, Hank knew this woman reminded him of someone. It was at that very moment, the outlaw leader recalled who that someone was.

"You are welcome, Mr. Metcalf. As for a woman preparing your meals, perhaps it's time for you to consider another line of work, something other than herding cows, I mean," Sarah replied, hoping Hank didn't read too much into her unwise and pointed statement.

"Maybe I should, ma'am, but surely you know by now that the choices one makes often render it impossible for a person to follow another path," he said, taking a small sip of his hot coffee. "Nothing personal, but perhaps you've experienced that truth in your own life as well."

Sarah winced, realizing Metcalf had inadvertently struck on a painful reality of her life and marriage to Ben Crenshaw.

"By the way, that's some fine coffee, Mrs. Crenshaw. And if you would pardon me for being so bold, I knew you put me to mind of someone. It took me a couple of hours, but I just figured it out."

As they spoke, she gazed into a pair of eyes that reminded Sarah of her dead husband, Ben. His eyes once sparkled with laughter and kindness too, while also hiding an inner cruelty and darkness that only her father ever saw and detected.

Like her departed father, she too came to see the evil in Ben's Crenshaw's eyes, much too late. But Sarah's eyes were open now and she recognized that same reckless danger in the person of Hank Metcalf.

"Okay, Mr. Metcalf, I have to admit that I'm curious. Who is it?"

"My mother, ma'am. You remind me of my dearly departed mother," he said, smiling. "And I mean that as the highest form of compliment."

"Well, I thank you then. You go now, eat up before your food gets cold. Sam and I will eat something too, before I tidy things back up."

As Hank walked away, it pained him that he never met a woman like this one in his youth, back before his life went off the straight and narrow. Things might have turned out differently and he wouldn't be constantly living under the fear of being captured and hanged.

At the same time, Metcalf recognized that everything was not what it seemed with Mrs. Crenshaw. Hank knew she was lying about her husband meeting them. And what kind of husband would send his wife and child into these conditions alone? Then there were the blood stains on her dress. Although he had no doubts that Mrs. Crenshaw was a fine woman, it was apparent to Metcalf that she was definitely hiding something.

That, however, was the least of Hank's worries, knowing that Braxton Poole and another lawman were already hot on his trail.

As Sarah prepared the plates for her and Sam, she watched Hank walk away and sit down next to Bill Ford. Sarah pretended that his behavior held no interest, as Metcalf began saying something to Ford, obviously speaking in hushed tones that could not be heard from where she was standing.

While carrying his food and coffee back toward where Ford was sitting, Metcalf noticed the outlaw staring at Mrs. Crenshaw like a kid eyeing stick candy in a general store. Now that Ford had satisfied his appetites for water and food, his mind turned to other urges that were yet to be sated.

"I'm telling you, Bill. Not this one, you don't," Hank whispered, firmly. "There's something about this Crenshaw woman that reminds me of my mother. I won't have her hurt, you understand me? Along with that, it might come down to a situation that we need her as a hostage."

"But I want her."

"Yeah, I could see that from clear over there," Hank said, weary of these endless disputes with Ford, whose uncontrollable appetites were quickly making him more of a disability than an asset. Metcalf was still angry with Bill for his foolhardy stunt with the whiskey, something else that could have left him one man short. "Mrs. Crenshaw could probably see it too. Leave her alone, Bill. That's an order."

"Yeah, I hear you," the outlaw grunted, the indifference in his tone lost on no one.

As Hank enjoyed his food, Ford's eyes returned to Mrs. Crenshaw, who was eating her meal while sitting alongside her son. His mind turned to the other women he had and the pleasures this one could offer him.

Ford suspected that his boss' concern for the woman wasn't strictly innocent on his part. No doubt Hank was only interested in keeping Crenshaw for himself. *No matter*, he thought. Ford determined that he would have this woman for his own before the day was out, even if it meant killing Metcalf to make it happen.

* * *

For the first time in weeks, clouds began to fill the sky above them, huge, gray puffy clouds, that delivered gallons and gallons of rain, which would take arid, dusty stream beds and swell them far beyond their banks.

Poole had seen their false promises of rain before, often when the weather brought about these bitter and endless droughts. Poole doubted that these clouds would bring about any break from these miserable conditions either. He removed his sweat-stained hat, loosed the bandana from around his neck, and dried his scroungy forehead.

"Are you ready now?" Olsen asked.

"You bet I am. Let's end this."

For only a moment, he considered the liquid refreshment that might be waiting for a man at Webster Springs. The idea certainly appealed to him. Then, Poole dismissed the notion as quickly as it came, because he had no time or patience for silly daydreams.

Although the going was slow and tedious, the two marshals made considerable progress, leaving them only a couple hundred yards away from the unsuspecting outlaws. When they talked, moments that were now rare, they spoke in low whispers.

Using the shadows, rocks, and vegetation as cover, often crawling on their bellies, much the same way as the Apaches often crept up on their victims, the two lawmen continued their painstaking advance on their targets. To Poole's relief, Olsen nudged his friend in the ribs and pointed toward Crenshaw and her son, confirming that the two of them were still unharmed.

Poole smiled, while also lifting his right thumb above his fist, signaling to Olsen his pleasure about seeing Sarah and Sam still alive. But Poole also accepted the fact that they were still not out of the woods yet. There were many dangers yet to be faced and harm could come to any one of them, with scarcely a moment's notice.

The marshal also knew that any kind of an error on their part could alert Metcalf and his gang to their position. Moreover, those odds grew infinitely greater with every foot of ground they covered.

Upon seeing Poole nod to him, Olsen signaled that he was veering off in his own direction. It was a plan that was mutually agreed upon, just before the two marshals set out the rest of the way on foot.

The lawmen planned to attack the outlaws from different directions, increasing their odds of killing two of the bandits with their first shots. Their strategy, if successful, might also result in one of the marshals being close enough to lead Mrs. Crenshaw and her son to safety, just as soon as their guns created a distraction.

It was decided between them that, before opening fire, they would allow enough time for each man to get into position outside the enemy's camp. In order so they didn't waste shells on the same individual, they agreed that each marshal would target the outlaw closest to them. Since Poole was clearly the better man with a rifle, he would be the one to start the ball rolling. Olsen would immediately follow his lead.

The two men were fully cognizant of the fact that one, or perhaps both of them, might die in carrying out this mission. And although the two friends were vastly different in personalities, they were completely united in their devotion to fulfilling their oaths of office and respecting the duties and responsibilities an individual took on himself while wearing the badge.

Poole took one final glance at Olsen and muttered underneath his breath, "Good luck, my friend."

Then he resumed the difficult chore of crawling within striking distance of the deadly outlaws' camp.

Chapter Twenty-One

Not more than a couple of hours after he rolled over on his side with plans of sleeping until nightfall, Kicking Deer was awakened by the sounds of movement, not too far from his own location. Familiar with nearly all of the sounds made by the area's wildlife, he decided the noises could only be made by a human.

Curious as to what they might be, he waited and watched.

It was then he saw Marshal Poole and the other lawman carefully stalking the other bunch of White devils. For just a moment, he admired their efforts, doing their best to imitate the actions of his own Apache warriors in battle.

It amused him to watch.

Then, Kicking Deer reached the conclusion that this newest situation might offer him even more horses to steal. Perhaps it would also give him a chance to test Poole in battle. For now, however, Kicking Deer was simply content to watch the Whites seeking to kill some of their own.

It was a situation that Kicking Deer was confident would have also brought a smile to the face of Victorio.

He did find the circumstances somewhat disturbing, because it wasn't only bad enough that they were trying to pin up his people on a reservation; now an Apache couldn't even find a comfortable spot to lay one's head in the wilderness without white men also encroaching on his territory.

But that is not what troubled him most of all.

No doubt this would be another evening when Blue Dove would wait for his return to camp, only to be disappointed when he didn't.

He hated leaving her with the fear that Kicking Deer had somehow been killed and joined his forebears.

Knowing he would soon be discovered by Poole if he remained in the same location, Kicking Deer also began approaching the camp, under cover. Once there, he would choose a spot where he could remain undiscovered, waiting until an opportunity to kill the Whites presented itself.

* * *

When it appeared that the outlaws trusted her enough to allow her to move around the camp freely, Sarah was already taking actions to facilitate her escape.

Along with her own canteen, she stole one of those that belonged to Metcalf's men as well. Under the guise of cleaning up, Sarah also snatched up some of their food and provisions, enough to get them through another couple of days.

Sneaking one last look at the outlaws to make sure that things were clear for her escape, Sarah could see that they were engrossed in a spirited game of poker. It was now or never, she decided, the moment she had been waiting for.

Sarah knew there was no way she could outrun them on horseback, so she decided her only chance for escape was to frighten away their mounts as she fled. Holding her finger up in front of her mouth, signaling Sam to be quiet, Sarah began rushing him along to where their horses were all picketed.

Her husband's pistol and rifle were already with her horse, but Sarah concealed a knife from dinner in the folds of her dress. Lifting Sam up onto the saddle, she was just getting ready to cut the other horses free, when she was suddenly startled by a sound from just behind her.

Sarah turned around to see the dark bores of three revolvers pointed at her middle.

Holding them were Hank Metcalf, Sid Russell, and Bill Ford.

"Why, shame on you, Mrs. Crenshaw," Hank said, his eyes dancing with an evil brand of humor as he spoke. "Maybe you really don't remind me that much of my sweet mother. After all, Ma would have never run out without saying her goodbyes first. That's not very good manners, is it, boys?"

Russell simply smiled and nodded. Ford made no expression except for the sadistic leers, directed at the woman's figure.

"Now, you get the boy," Hank said, directing her towards the horse with the barrel of his gun, "and come on back to the fire with us."

Knowing Metcalf had the situation under control, Sid holstered his gun, walking on back to the fire and to his cup of coffee. Ford followed him, but constantly kept throwing a suspicious glance over his shoulder at Hank and the woman.

"And Mrs. Crenshaw, I'll be needing you to hand back over that knife you're holding, handle first, if you don't mind."

Reluctantly, Sarah placed the knife in his outstretched hand, while he trained his gun on her with the other. Upon receiving the knife, Metcalf smiled and holstered his revolver. "Much better, ma'am. I just wanted to dissuade you from trying anything cute with that blade. Now, you walk."

Leading the boy close in front of her, Sarah ambled back towards the camp. Looking back over her shoulder, she said, "What tipped you off to watch me, Mr. Metcalf?"

He laughed. "I suppose it was those blood stains on your dress, Mrs. Crenshaw. Not too many women I know would leave the house looking that way. It made me speculate that you had to leave in a hurry."

Sarah, still a little ashamed of her actions and not wishing to share them with anybody, made no effort to explain her business to a stranger, especially one who was holding them against her will.

"Now I have a question for you, ma'am."

Sarah nodded.

"What gave us away?"

She stopped and turned around to face the outlaw's leader. "You claimed you were a bunch of drifting cowhands, Mr. Metcalf, but your men spent way too much of the time checking their guns. And since random bovine attacks are rather uncommon, I thought your caution was somewhat extreme. Besides, I heard some talk around town about a killer named Metcalf."

Metcalf threw back his head and laughed. "Damned if I don't like you, ma'am. You've got sand and a smart mouth, both good qualities in a woman.

"You have no real reason to believe me, Mrs. Crenshaw, but it is my intention that no harm should come to you or your boy. All I ask is that you don't cause us any more anxieties and keep your head down when the shooting starts. Can you do that?"

"Shooting?"

"Yes, there might be some shooting when the marshals arrive. You should be fine if you stay down."

Now, she was curious. "Marshals? Coming here?"

"Yes, ma'am, some marshal named Braxton Poole and the other one is Miles Olsen, I think. They've been on our trail for some time now. Like us, like you, they'll be needing water. I plan to kill the two of them and then we can both be on our way. I'm sure they'll hit us after the sun goes down."

Marshal Poole is coming here? The thought of it offered Sarah a degree of hope, but the idea also left her afraid that some form of harm would come to this kind and decent lawman.

At the sound of their names, Sarah had done her best to reveal nothing as to her particular knowledge of either one of them.

As much as she wanted to see Marshal Poole and her thoughts returned to him much over the past couple days, she feared that those feelings would never be reciprocated.

If Poole wasn't killed by Metcalf and his men, perhaps he would do nothing but arrest Sarah for killing her husband. And what interest would an upright lawman ever take in a convicted killer?

Sarah wondered what kind of depraved woman she must be to conceive these kind of thoughts less than two days after she took the life of her husband. Even though her actions were only prompted by the desire to protect her son, Sarah still believed herself a monster for taking the life of Sam's father.

Theirs had been a good marriage at one time, or so she thought. Sarah even loved Ben once, with all her heart. But that was before she discovered the truth about Ben killing her parents. These many hours with only herself to depend on had made the situation abundantly clear to her; Ben Crenshaw never really loved her.

He only wanted to possess Sarah, to have someone to share his bed at night. Their union had amounted to little more than heartache and violence.

Although it pained her to acknowledge the fact, nothing good ever came from their marriage, nothing except for the birth of her precious son, Sam.

"What if the marshals capture you and your men?" Sarah asked him.

"That won't happen."

"How can you be so sure? You don't control fate, Mr. Metcalf."

"But we do control ours, ma'am. We've all pretty well decided that we won't allow ourselves to go to the gallows. Kill or be killed, those are the choices our paths in life have determined. Okay, let's get on back now," Hank said, with a smile, "before Bill starts to worry about us."

Sarah continued walking back towards the camp, still uncertain of what Hank Metcalf meant by his remark. But if it involved the person of Bill Ford, Sarah feared to learn more.

* * *

Only about an hour before nightfall, Marshal Poole had finally worked his way into position. From his place of concealment, he could see Sarah and the others sitting around the campfire. Once more, Poole was pleased when it appeared no harm had yet befallen Sarah or the boy.

Now that he was here, the marshal determined that none would.

No less than twice, the lawman had placed his rifle sights on the miserable skull of Bill Ford, but Poole feared to pull the trigger, speculating that Olsen wasn't fully in position to strike.

Poole knew if he shot too early, Olsen wouldn't be able to single out Metcalf, leaving the outlaw leader with time to harm Sarah. If he waited too long, the chance to save Sarah and her son might be lost forever. And that outcome was something that Poole didn't even dare to consider.

With each passing moment, Poole's patience declined and his fears for the Crenshaws increased. Checking his watch, Poole figured he would give it another ten minutes before he struck. Even if Olsen failed to make it into position, perhaps he could still take out Ford and Metcalf with two quick shots. Poole knew he must try.

As the minutes slowly ticked off from his watch, Poole reluctantly watched the outlaws and waited for his time to strike, but the lawman had no way of knowing that he was now all alone in this mission.

Chapter Twenty-Two

Although he was about twenty years older than Braxton Poole, Miles Olsen was strong and healthy beyond his years. The trek had been a tough one for the aging lawman, but it was nothing he hadn't done many times in the recent past.

Olsen was a fine lawman and a superb tracker, qualities which served him well over the years, long after he walked away from his service with the Texas Rangers, when he was catching horse and cattle thieves and pursuing border bandits.

Miles' wife, Martha, often lovingly urged him to resign, but he wasn't sure how they would make a living without his marshal's salary. It wasn't that they didn't have the money to get by; they did. It was just that Olsen could never seem to get over his fear of the unforeseen, a habit he somehow didn't apply to instances such as this one.

On this occasion, the seasoned marshal was crawling on his belly through the dirt, trying to keep his rifle clean, while also hoping he wouldn't be noticed by the ones he was fixing to kill. It was a tall order for a young man, even more so for one of his age.

Despite that fact, he and Poole covered almost a mile and a half on foot and stalked the last few hundred yards on their bellies without being seen. They did all this on a limited supply of water. Like Poole, Olsen was determined to save the woman and her son, although he didn't share some of Braxton's personal motivations.

In his years as a lawman, Olsen didn't miss much. He didn't miss anything this time either, his startled eyes carefully examining the moccasin print, which resembled that of the Apache brave they tracked earlier.

Upon seeing it, Olsen knew the two of them were in deep trouble. Moreover, the Indian's presence placed all of them in danger. As good as he was on a trail, Miles was dreadfully aware that the Apaches were better.

Because of his close proximity to the outlaws' camp, Olsen knew he didn't dare call out for help. Unsure of where the Indian brave was located and knowing Poole was counting on his guns for support, Miles couldn't turn back.

The situation left the lawman with few good options.

Uncertain of what else to do than make an attempt to complete their mission, Olsen swallowed hard and continued forward, his eyes darting back and forth, hoping to spot any sign or movement from a skilled and deadly adversary he knew had to be somewhere close.

Much too close.

* * *

Approximately an hour before the sunset, the formerly thirsty travelers were sitting around the campfire. Because the outlaws potentially needed her as a hostage and since she already attempted an escape, Sarah wasn't permitted to leave their sight.

She sat next to the campfire, her hand resting on the back of her son, who already drifted off to sleep for the night. While she appeared to be complacent for now, Sarah's mind never stopped working on plans to get away. She also wanted to do whatever she could to assist Marshal Poole whenever he might choose to attack.

Despite Metcalf's assurances that she would not be harmed, the soulless and lustful eyes of Bill Ford continued to frighten Sarah. They never seemed to go anywhere else. Those fears weren't only for her, but also carried over to the life of her son.

Sid Russell leaned back on his saddle and said, "Do you remember what you told me back there, Hank?"

"Back there?" he replied. "What are you talking about, Sid?"

"Yeah, back when we were still searching for water. You remember, don't you, Hank? You told me if I found water for us, then you would tell me the story about your connection to Marshal Poole."

Hank took another drink of coffee. "I suppose you're right. I did tell you that." Before starting, he threw back his head and laughed, as one often does while recalling a fond or embarrassing memory of the past.

Above all else, Metcalf was a master storyteller. Perhaps even more than his desire to never return to prison, he loved to share stories of his own escapes or misadventures, along with listening to those being told by others.

"Well, it happened right after I robbed my first bank. It was Marshal Poole who was sent out to arrest me. I think he was about as green to his profession as I was to mine.

"Later I learned, it took him almost four months to pick up my trail. From the look of things now, it would appear that Poole's learned a few things since then," he continued. "And when he comes this time, Poole may see that I've learned a few new tricks, too."

Russell, now standing over next to the fire, used a gloved hand to remove the coffee pot from the fire. He poured himself another cup and said, "Go on, boss."

"Anyway, there was this little cantina on the border I used to frequent, with a dark-eyed senorita who kind of fancied me." Hank smiled as he recalled the woman and their numerous trysts in his mind. "Josita, that was her name. A wild little thing, she was, full of piss and tequila. You know what I'm talking about, Sid, the kind of woman who makes a man forget about everything except getting back to her again."

"Yeah, boss, I know."

"Come to think of it, I might just head on back that way after this is all over. I'm a mite curious to see if that dark-eyed Josita is still working there. Maybe she's still as wild as I remember."

"Go on, boss. What happened?"

"I don't have to tell you how hot it is down there. The bed sheets were soaked with sweat, from both the daytime heat and the special kind of attention that Josita generally gave to her men. As I recall, it was a Sunday morning when Poole found me. I remember it well, because the church bells were ringing down the street at the Catholic mission.

"You'll pardon me, ma'am, but I'll be damned if it wasn't those church bells that did me in," Hank continued. "Between her screams and the noise off those church bells, I didn't hear anything when Poole started shooting it out with two of my boys, downstairs. And I was kind of distracted, if you know what I mean.

"I barely had time to buckle on my gun belt, before he kicked in the door. Come to think of it, a gun belt was just about all I was wearing when I first met Braxton Poole, that and my socks. Still had my socks on, I did. I must have been a sight. Poole even laughed about it, while holding that big gun of his on me the whole time."

The members of Metcalf's gang chortled heartily at Hank's story, but Ford soon returned his attentions back to Sarah Crenshaw and the secrets of her figure that no dress could ever fully conceal.

"I thought about drawing on Poole," Metcalf said, "but for some reason I didn't. That won't happen the next time we meet. You can be certain of that."

Ford had long since lost interest in Hank's story. He was only concerned with the rancher's wife and the pleasures her body offered any man bold enough to take her for his own.

Bill knew Hank Metcalf wasn't a fool. Despite his earlier warnings to leave Mrs. Crenshaw alone, Ford knew that Hank would be needing his guns when the time came to face the pair of marshals. Metcalf and Ford needed each other. With that consideration in mind, Bill speculated that Hank didn't dare kill Ford for acting on his impulses with the Crenshaw woman, as long as she was still alive afterwards.

Alive, but a little used, Ford reasoned, *didn't make Crenshaw any less valuable as a hostage.*

"Sid, is there any more of that coffee?" Ford said, using the statement as a ruse for his true intentions.

"Yes, there is," Russell replied. "You want me to get you some?"

"No, I got it," the big outlaw muttered, holding the coffee cup in his left hand, while also drawing his gun and hiding it behind his right hip. As Bill strode over behind Hank, seemingly like he was headed towards the fire, Ford hammered his boss across the skull with the barrel of his pistol.

Metcalf, who failed to anticipate the attack coming, went down in a heap.

Ford dropped his coffee cup and sprang for the woman. Bill caught hold of the startled woman's arm with his left hand, dragging her, kicking and screaming to the edge of the camp, all the while keeping his gun hand free to confront any challenge.

Russell sprang to his feet to stop him, but Bill pointed his gun at the younger outlaw. "You sit back down there and drink your coffee, or I'll kill you, Sid, I already owe you one anyway," he muttered, almost lifting and carrying the frightened Mrs. Crenshaw off for his own pleasure.

Sarah screamed and beat upon his chest, but her strength was no match for the burly outlaw, whose carnal intentions were no longer to be doubted.

* * *

Upon seeing the two lawmen sneaking up on the camp, Kicking Deer knew this situation presented much too good an opportunity to pass up. Choosing rather to engage Poole later, the Indian decided that now was the time to begin inflicting some retribution to these numerous white invaders.

Kicking Deer drew his blade and began inching forward, approaching his target from behind, quickly closing the distance on Poole's friend.

Even the Apache brave found himself impressed by the lawman's unusual skills on the trail. From the man's behavior, Kicking Deer could tell that Olsen had become aware of his presence and was continually watching for him to appear.

Most of the warrior's white victims never knew he was anywhere around them before he took their lives.

Despite the man's best efforts, Kicking Deer was more than a match for the aging lawman. When Kicking Deer thought the moment was right, he struck like a rattlesnake, springing atop the crawling man's back, choking off any sounds that might come from his mouth as his sharp blade raked across Olsen's white throat.

Olsen merely laid there after the attack, as his crimson, life's blood began to pour out upon the dusty soil. Kicking Deer continued to hold his hand over the lawman's mouth, to keep his final gasping sounds from being heard by the others, who were only mere yards from his victim.

In his final moments upon this earth, gazing at the bloody soil beneath him, Miles thought of his precious wife, Martha, his sons, and his fifteen grandchildren. In words that would never be heard by anybody and which passed only through his mind, Olsen apologized to his family for the grief which would come with his passing.

Miles drew his final breath in a state of shame, believing that he ultimately failed to assist his friend, Braxton Poole, and he feared that good people would die from it.

His body then went limp and still.

Kicking Deer placed his bloody blade at the base of Olsen's scalp and deftly claimed another trophy to add to his collection. The Apache smiled at his good fortune and moved on to collect more scalps.

Chapter Twenty-Three

Frantically checking his watch for the tenth time in the past thirty seconds, Poole could see there were only two minutes remaining of the ten he allotted for Miles to get into position.

Despite his impulsive need to act now, the marshal knew that Sarah's best chance at being safely rescued would require him to remain calm and stick to their plan.

Throughout their many years of friendship, Poole could always count on Miles Olsen, whenever they were taking down outlaws, to do exactly what they discussed. He expected nothing less this time.

His patience nearly at its end, Poole cast a wistful and fleeting glance towards the peaceful and inviting waters of Webster Springs, but he knew his thirst was something that would have to wait.

The pair of innocent lives at stake made that one desire a low priority.

It was then he saw Bill Ford rise to his feet and begin walking towards the fire, a situation that Poole believed would make Ford a much easier target for Olsen's gun, leaving his rifle free to take down Metcalf.

Poole licked his lips, figuring this was precisely the scenario the two marshals hoped for while formulating their plans.

What happened next took everybody by surprise, from those in his own gang, to Sarah Crenshaw, and especially for the United States Marshal who was waiting to kill the outlaw, Bill Ford.

Ford's unforeseen attack on Metcalf immediately prompted the marshal to act, even if Olsen had failed to reach his position. This situation left Poole with no other choice. With Hank momentarily out of the fight and Ford's assault on the woman immediately placing

Sarah in danger, Poole threw the Winchester to his shoulder and began seeking a target on which to fire. But just as he was taking up slack on his trigger, Ford started dragging Sarah to the edge of camp, exposing her to danger from any shot he might risk.

For just a moment, Poole wondered what might have delayed his friend. *This isn't like Miles,* he thought. He knew Sarah's screams should have alerted Miles, but he instantly recalled something he learned in the war, that a man was often stronger in battle when relying only on himself.

To hell with Miles, Poole thought. *I must save Sarah.*

* * *

After pulling the screaming woman beyond the camp, Ford, who now grew weary of the woman's cries for help, slapped Sarah across the mouth, knocking her much smaller body into the dust.

Ford desired to exercise his vile affections with Sarah Crenshaw from the very first moment he saw her.

Now he would.

Pleased with himself and smiling in triumph, Ford advanced in her direction, figuring he already harmed the rancher's wife enough to ensure her compliance. He quickly discovered she was much tougher than the other women he forced his attentions upon, when, despite her injuries, Sarah scrambled to her feet and raced away.

Cursing and threatening to kill the woman when he caught her, Bill sprinted after Sarah, who was much faster than he imagined. Finally pulling within arm's reach of her, but still unable to run her down, he placed his hand on her back and shoved. The forward momentum of her body sent her flying face-first into the dust.

Towering above her, Ford now determined that he would deal more harshly with Sarah than he originally planned. He tugged at his gun belt, loosing his gun and letting it fall to the ground. While moving towards the woman, Bill fumbled at his pants, before pinning her to the ground with his hulking frame.

Ford fondled and pawed at her legs and hips, growing furious at her attempts to restrain him. Determined to bring the woman into submission, Bill slapped her twice, ripping at her clothes, tearing the meager dress that covered Sarah's body.

Revolted by the man's brutal attempts to rape her, Sarah fought, kicked, and screamed with every ounce of strength and courage she could muster. She detested Ford's foul breath upon her lips as he feverishly struggled to kiss her.

Crenshaw's protests and resistance only made the experience more exciting for Bill, who took great pleasure in the process of subduing the women who made their violations challenging.

Sarah viciously bit his lower lip until she drew blood, causing the outlaw to scream like a wounded animal. This action earned her another brutal, open palm slap across her jaw from his massive right hand, a blow which left her shaken and reeling on the edge of consciousness.

Just about the time when Ford thought he was about to have his way with Sarah, he heard shooting from inside the camp. Cursing at his bad luck, Ford guessed that it had to be an attack from those two relentless marshals.

Figuring he could claim the Crenshaw woman anytime, Bill sprang from the ground and dashed over to find his gun belt.

* * *

His slumber disturbed by the sudden movements and the loud shouting, Sam awoke, bewildered about his mother's unexplained absence. Then he heard Sarah's screams and called out for his mother, transforming him into a lonely, frightened child in a strange place.

Like any child in the same situation, Sam broke into tears.

With Hank unconscious, a boy crying, and Ford off to himself, defiling another handsome woman, Sid Russell was instantly at a loss as to what he should do.

Unwilling to wait for Olsen any longer and unsure of how he should respond as well, Marshal Poole took a deep breath, scrambled to his feet, and charged into the outlaws' camp.

Sid Russell, startled by the marshal's sudden appearance, palmed his gun and snapped off two quick shots at Poole. Shooting too quickly, both of his slugs failed to hit their intended target.

The same could not be said for Poole. Firing the rifle from his hip, Poole's blast failed to hit anything vital. The slug tore a bloody crease along Russell's side. Painful but not serious enough to stop him, the outlaw remained on his feet and raised his gun once again in the direction of the marshal. Poole met this latest threat with calmness and precision, triggering a shot that caught the bandit squarely in the chest.

The heavy rifle slug sent Russell's body reeling, driving him backwards against the fire. Sid was dead before he hit the ground. The flames caught Sid's left shirt sleeve ablaze. As the fire began to spread to the rest of his clothes, Russell felt no pain.

With one of the outlaws unconscious for now and the other one dead, Poole's first concern was caring for the safety of Sarah's son. He scooped the boy into his arms at a dead run and carried him back to the place where he'd just been hiding.

"Sam," he said, "you remember me. I'm Marshal Poole; we met once in town. You recall that?"

The boy nodded, wiping the tears from his eyes.

"Good, Sam. I have to go help your mother now. You stay right here and keep hidden until I get back. Can you do that?"

"Yes," he said, "you can count on me, sir."

"Good boy," Poole replied, tousling the hair on the child's head. "Don't go anywhere. You wait for me here," he stated once again, before dashing off with his Winchester to help Sarah.

As Poole sprinted outside the camp, racing towards the sounds of Sarah's tortured screams, he paused when he encountered the dead body of Miles Olsen.

Poole's throat grew tight and he swallowed hard at the sight of his friend and fallen lawman.

Olsen's throat had been cut and he had been scalped, which could mean only one thing. The Indian who killed the young gambler back at the Crenshaw ranch was right here among them.

A single moccasin track next to the body confirmed it.

And now Poole was faced with realization that there lurked one more individual nearby who was out to kill them.

He cursed softly.

Believing that Miles Olsen was deserving of a much better fate in this life, Poole knew there was nothing to be done for him right now. His responsibility rested solely with preserving the living.

Sarah Crenshaw was still alive and alone.

And she needed help.

* * *

Sarah, still hurting from the beating she received, was relieved when Ford strangely halted his assault. She, too, had heard the sound of gunfire, figuring that the marshals had begun their attack.

"I'll be back for you, darling. We'll finish this later," Ford cruelly stated, while rushing to retrieve his revolver.

Before Ford could pick up his gun, Kicking Deer charged him from out of the shadows, but a huge right hand knocked the Apache brave to the ground. Seeing what the Indian had in mind for him, Ford seemed almost pleased to display his fighting skills in front of the woman.

Bill grabbed his own knife to engage the Indian.

"I am Kicking Deer," the Indian said, proudly. "It is good to know the name of the one who will take your scalp."

Having said that, the two men went blade to blade.

Upon seeing the pair fighting, Sarah recognized that her life would continue to be in danger, no matter who prevailed in this deadly struggle. Unsure of which one of them most deserved the term, "savage," Sarah determined that Ford would never get the opportunity to finish what he started with her.

She would die first.

Or he would.

Unwilling to be victimized again, she gladly seized the opportunity to snatch up Bill's fallen gun belt and weapon. Sarah also thought she might need the gun in order to fight her way back to her son and ensure his own safety.

Springing to his feet, Kicking Deer slashed and cut at the outlaw, who somehow briefly managed to elude his fierce attacks. Despite the Indian's experience, it was Ford who drew first blood, leaving a bloody stripe across the warrior's bare chest. Kicking Deer, however, was a veteran of hand-to-hand fighting and welcomed this challenge.

Feinting and slashing, they danced around each other for a time. Kicking Deer darted and parried, cutting a gash across the bigger man's forearm. The fight continued for only a few more brief moments, before Kicking Deer finally defeated Ford in a furious rush, plunging the knife deep within his chest.

Having buried the blade in his adversary, driving it clear up to the hilt, the Indian smiled as he wrenched it free.

Ford, unaccustomed to losing any kind of a battle, stared at the grievous wound that Kicking Deer inflicted upon him. The outlaw's eyes grew large. Disbelievingly, he gazed at the bloody knife held by his opponent.

Like a drunkard, Ford swayed on his feet for a moment, before the huge man tumbled face first into the dust. While he was still breathing, Kicking Deer took his knife and peeled away the scalp from his head.

Pleased that her attacker had been killed, Sarah knew that Bill Ford's death didn't mean she was out of danger. The threat just took on a different form and face.

Thinking that he would kill two white victims at nearly the same time and place, Kicking Deer marveled at his good fortune. He started towards the woman with the bloody knife in his hand.

Without any hesitancy whatsoever, Sarah pulled back the hammer and fired a slug through the Apache's left shoulder. Realizing he'd been foolish to take the woman's willingness to fight for granted, and also forgetting the admonitions of his father, the wound only served to outrage Kicking Deer.

As Kicking Deer readied himself to make another run at the woman, Marshal Poole came rushing to the scene. Seeing Poole raising the rifle to his shoulder, the Indian darted into the shadows, as the shot from the rifle scarcely missed the Apache.

"Are you all right, Sarah? Did Ford hurt you?" he asked.

A quick examination of the injuries to her face told Poole that Sarah had suffered terribly at the hands of Bill Ford. But fortunately, the deadly outlaw had failed in his attempts to harm her any worse. And when Sarah tried to cover herself from where her dress had been partially torn, Poole failed miserably in his lofty goal to avert his eyes.

He blushed when Sarah saw him.

"No, I'm fine," she replied, pretending not to notice.

"I'm glad."

Confident that the Indian had indeed fled, Poole offered his hand to Sarah, to lift her from the ground. Once she came to her feet, Sarah threw out her arms and embraced the lawman firmly.

"Thank you, Marshal," she said.

"You're welcome, Sarah."

Despite the awkwardness of being in the arms of a woman other than his late wife, Poole enjoyed the moment and returned Sarah's embrace as fully as he received it. Moreover, that feeling was not missed by the woman.

As they parted, he said, "From what I could see of the situation, it looks like you already had things well in hand."

"I'm not sure what would have happened if you hadn't shown up, Marshal. The Indian had little problem killing Bill Ford. He even identified himself first. He called himself Kicking Deer."

Poole nodded his head at the mention of the name. "I've heard of him. He's a bad one, all right. Runs with Victorio. He already murdered Miles Olsen, just over there a ways," he said, pointing in the direction of his friend.

Sarah hung her head at the news and a tear came to her eye. "I'm so sorry about your friend. He died trying to help me."

"At least his death had some value, then," Poole observed. "Miles knew what he was getting into, but that doesn't make it go down any easier."

Despite the cuts and bruises, and without any means to care for her hair and features for days, Poole thought Sarah Crenshaw was quite likely one of the most strikingly handsome women he ever saw.

"Where is Sam?" she blurted out. "Is he safe?"

"He should be," the marshal said. "I hid him away before I came to help you. Until we know you're safe, you need to try and stay behind me, Sarah. But be sure and keep that gun handy," he warned. "Hank Metcalf is still out there. So is Kicking Deer."

"You lead the way, Marshal," Sarah said. "I'm right behind you. Let's go find my son."

Chapter Twenty-Four

As Poole led Sarah back to the camp, he deliberately guided her away from the dead and mutilated remains of his friend, Miles Olsen. The marshal figured it was bad enough that he had to see what Kicking Deer did to him; he didn't believe Sarah needed to have that image locked in her mind the rest of her life.

As they entered the camp, the air reeked of burnt flesh and fabric, scents left behind from where Russell had died, his left arm falling into the flames and the fire removing a portion of the clothes from his body.

Using the toe of his boot, Poole shoved Russell's body away from the flames. The scene was a ghastly one and Sarah turned away her eyes from the sight of it.

Poole stooped down to pick up one of the blankets and threw it over the body. It did nothing to cover Russell's charred and outstretched arm. He caught up another one of the outlaws' blankets and handed it to Sarah.

"You can use this to fully cover yourself."

Sarah smiled and thanked him.

With her mind focused on nothing but her son, Sarah called out for him, and Sam came running from his place of concealment. Sarah caught up the boy in her arms and squeezed the child and kissed his cheeks. It was a moment she never expected to have again, after Ford snatched her away from the camp.

After she was done loving on her son, Sam took his place right next to her.

It was just about that minute when they saw that Hank Metcalf was first beginning to stir. As he rose to his feet, Hank rubbed the knot on his head, a painful reminder of the blow that he received from the barrel of Ford's gun.

Any thoughts of challenging the marshal were immediately dismissed from Hank's mind when he saw Poole's Winchester leveled at his chest. Metcalf also knew that now was not the time for gun play, after just returning to consciousness.

Metcalf glanced over towards the campfire and saw the smoldering remains of Sid Russell.

Poole went ahead and answered the question in the outlaw's eyes before Hank ever had a chance to ask it.

"Sid left me no choice, Hank. He drew his gun on me."

Metcalf nodded. "What about Bill?"

"You'll find Ford's body out there, not too far from where we're standing," Poole explained. "He tried to have his way with the woman. His plans for Sarah were thwarted when Ford was killed and scalped by a renegade Apache."

"An Indian? Out here?"

"Yes, his name is Kicking Deer. Runs with Victorio," Poole said. "There's little doubt that he planned to murder and scalp the whole bunch of you while you slept and then steal your horses when he was done."

"Sounds like I missed a passel of things while I was napping," Metcalf replied, as he shook his head to clear away the cobwebs. "Bill Ford killed by an Indian, I never saw that one coming. I always said that his ungodly urges for women would be the death of him eventually. Guess it finally done him in."

"By the way, Mrs. Crenshaw, I'm sorry for the harm that came to you," Hank continued. "I never meant for that to happen. I even told Ford to leave you alone."

"That's enough of your lies," Sarah blurted out. "Don't try to minimize your involvement in all of this."

"My involvement?"

"Yes, Mr. Metcalf, *your* involvement. You knew all about Bill Ford. You rode with him. You knew what Ford did to women in the past. That makes you as guilty as he is," Sarah said, still clinging to the pistol she removed from Ford's dropped gun belt. "I don't need a man to waste my time with phony apologies, absent of any genuine remorse. I've already experienced enough of that for two lifetimes."

"Yes, indeed, she's a tough one, Marshal," Hank said, looking at Poole while once again wishing he met Sarah Crenshaw much earlier in his life.

It's those choices one makes again, he thought.

"You mind if I get my hat, Poole?"

"Not if you do it real slow and easy."

As Metcalf bent over to retrieve his hat, he thought about going for his gun, but decided against it when he observed that the marshal's eyes and his rifle never wavered. Hank remained confident that other opportunities would present themselves.

One just had to seize them.

After returning the hat to his head, Hank turned to the marshal and said, "There, that's better. Now, what about me, Poole?"

"There's not much to tell. I'll be taking you back to stand trial, Hank."

"And you won't even give me a fair chance, will you, Marshal? Maybe you're afraid I might just take you."

"Perhaps," Poole said, "but why should I take the chance? I already have you in custody now. It doesn't make much sense for me to take any risks. Besides, I have to look after the safety of a woman and her child."

Hank smiled. "Look at it this way, Poole. After I kill you, I'll make certain that Mrs. Crenshaw and the boy make it safely back to town. You have my word on it. I'm just asking for a chance."

"No, Hank, that's not going to happen. I want you to slowly remove that gun with your left hand and toss it on the ground." Poole motioned with his rifle. "Do it now."

Certain that the marshal would never be persuaded, Hank relented and dropped his six-gun into the dust.

Always anxious to help an adult, Sam said, "I'll get it for you, Marshal," while rushing over to pick up the gun.

"No," Poole shouted, much too late to keep the child away from arm's reach of the outlaw.

Recognizing that this was the random opportunity for which he waited, Metcalf snatched up the boy, using him for a shield, while also retrieving his gun, the barrel of which he placed against Sam's head.

"Now, Marshal," Metcalf said, "it's time that we started doing things my way. And I'm sorry for this, Mrs. Crenshaw. I *do* like you, but not enough to go to the gallows for you, or even for my dearly departed mother."

Filled with nothing but rage and fear, Sarah longed to kill this man with the gun she was still holding. "As I said before, you can keep your empty promises, but if anything happens to Sam, I promise you, Mr. Metcalf, that I will kill you myself."

Hank laughed without humor. "Listen to her, Marshal. She sounds like she really means it."

Remembering the grim and bloody scene he discovered earlier, back at the Crenshaw ranch, Poole observed, "Trust me, Hank. She isn't kidding. Not in the least."

"Well, okay, Poole. Time's wasting here. What will it be? I don't want to hurt the boy, but I will if I have to."

The angry and frightened mother glared daggers at Metcalf.

The marshal held up his left hand in a sign of restraint. "All right, Hank, you win. If you promise not to hurt him, I'll give you a fair shot."

As much as she wanted safety for her son, Sarah also didn't wish to sacrifice the life of the marshal. "Please, Braxton, there has to be another way."

"There isn't, Sarah."

Knowing there was no other way to resolve this standoff, Poole's eyes moved away from Hank to those of the woman. "If Metcalf does kill me, Sarah, you make sure you don't turn loose of that gun, not until he gets you both to somewhere safe. Will you promise me that?"

With tears filling her eyes and unable to speak, Sarah only nodded.

Turning his attention back to the outlaw, Poole lowered his rifle and placed it on the ground next to him. Upon seeing this deliberate concession from the marshal, Hank holstered his gun and released the boy, who went running into the outstretched arms of his mother.

"Sarah, you take Sam and stand aside. I don't want either of you to get hurt."

Grudgingly, she consented to do as Poole had told them. Before moving, Sarah gently touched the marshal's face and ushered her son away from the line of fire, softly muttering, "There has to be another way."

Upon seeing to the Crenshaws' safety, Poole said, "You don't have to do this, Hank. You might even find a lawyer good enough to get you off."

"Do you really believe that, Poole?"

"I believe in the system."

"I don't."

For what seemed like an eternity to Sarah, the pair of men stood facing one another, the marshal and the outlaw, hands near the butts of their revolvers. Sarah longed for the gun fight to be over; she feared to see the results when it was.

"It's your move, Hank."

"Goodbye, Marshal," he replied, smiling.

Metcalf's hands flashed for his gun in an instant . . .

Hank's triumphant smile only vanished from his face when he realized that Poole's six-gun was already up and firing, his two individual shots sounding as one.

Sarah scarcely realized either of the men had drawn their guns, when a pair of deadly slugs pierced Hank's chest like glowing steel from a hot branding iron.

His gun finally coming level, the shot from Hank's pistol errantly rippled the once-peaceful waters of Webster Springs.

Metcalf staggered on his feet, and then pitched forward into the dust, the gun still clutched firmly in his lifeless fist.

Delighted that the danger was all behind them now, Sarah ran to the marshal's side. Before she had the chance to embrace him, she was stopped by a sound, coming from just outside the camp.

Poole wheeled around, bringing his gun to bear on this latest threat, only to be confronted by the face of the Indian, Kicking Deer, who was holding a rifle on them.

Chapter Twenty-Five

Upon seeing Kicking Deer, who had come for their horses, Sarah shoved her son behind her back to shield him from any danger. At the same moment, Poole also reached out with his left arm to usher Sarah behind him for safety as well.

Sarah wondered if she would ever again see a moment without danger.

A rifle pointed at Poole's chest and the marshal's six-gun leveled on the brave's midsection, they remained in that position until the Indian spoke.

"I am Kicking Deer."

Over time, the Apache acquired some limited knowledge of the English language. The words still sounded strange to him as they rolled off his tongue.

"I know who you are. What do you want?"

"You are the one they call 'Poole?'"

"I am."

"And Crenshaw is now your woman?"

Unsure of how to respond to the Indian's question, but fearing for Sarah's safety should he answer any other way, Poole said, "Yes, she is my woman."

Although Sarah fully understood why the marshal chose to answer Kicking Deer in the manner he did, she still found that it brought her some sense of satisfaction to hear him utter those words.

"Crenshaw is a strong woman and should raise many strong sons."

Sarah blushed slightly at that statement.

"Perhaps," Poole replied. "As I asked you before, Kicking Deer, what do you want here?"

"I come to claim four horses. I take those of the three men you killed and that belonging to Crenshaw."

Poole shook his head and held up two fingers on his left hand. "No, Kicking Deer, you take two horses. Two horses only. We keep the one Crenshaw rode. I need them to get these bodies back to town."

"Maybe I kill you, Poole, and take them all."

Poole thought he detected the hint of a smile on the warrior's face.

"You might try. But perhaps I kill you, Kicking Deer, and then you don't take any horses."

Kicking Deer simply stared at the man holding a gun on him. Gazing into the lawman's eyes, he detected no fear in them. "Two horses?"

"Yes, two horses. You already have the horse belonging to the man you killed at the Crenshaw ranch."

Sarah's eyes grew large at the mention of the ranch.

Not fully satisfied with the lawman's offer, Kicking Deer knew that returning with three horses and fresh scalps would make him a great warrior in his camp. It was also more than he needed to purchase Blue Dove's hand.

Knowing he was certain to have the woman he desired, Poole's deal would be enough, for now.

Sarah was now confident that Marshal Poole knew all about the murder of her husband, Ben. Perhaps he had come all this way with the other marshal to arrest her. The memory of her actions caused Sarah to hang her head in shame. She feared what would happen to her son, after her arrest.

Still, she knew nothing about the killing of another man back at their place. Apparently, much had happened there since she fled with Sam.

Upon Poole's mention of the young gambler he killed at the Crenshaw ranch, Kicking Deer's eyes lit up. "He was not a warrior, like your friend was."

Anger and bitterness rose inside Poole at the mention of the Indian's murder of Miles Olsen. Still, Poole knew for the sake of Sarah and Sam, it was important that he restrain himself, at least for now.

"You should take those two horses and go now," Poole said, sternly. "It is a good deal, the best one you're apt to find here today. Nothing else but death awaits you here."

The Indian nodded, satisfied with the compromise, which would leave him with two horses more than he needed to purchase Blue Dove. His raid had been a profitable one; he could now purchase the hand of his love.

Poole's death could wait for now.

"I take the two horses and go now," Kicking Deer said, lowering his rifle as he turned to walk away.

"Kicking Deer," Poole said, causing the Indian to pause and turn around, "you killed my friend, Miles Olsen. I will be coming for you. You can count on it."

The Apache's eyes showed no fear at the mention of those words. "I will welcome our meeting."

Following his comment, Kicking Deer simply smiled and walked away.

Still holding the six-gun in his hand, Poole followed Kicking Deer to where the horses were tied and only holstered the weapon when he confirmed the Apache was indeed gone.

Thinking of nothing else but making sure that Kicking Deer was safely departed from their midst, Poole failed to see the armed man who was now closing the distance between them.

Despite the deadly knife wound and the scalp that was now missing from his skull, somehow Bill Ford was still alive. His face and body were dirty and covered with caked blood, a dead man walking.

Driven by his rage and hatred, Ford raised his knife and was only ten feet away from plunging his weapon into the back of the distracted marshal.

Seeing she had no time to warn Marshal Poole and fearful for his life, Sarah raised her revolver and squeezed the trigger. Somewhere in the process, she screamed. The force of the slug loosed the blade from Ford's hand and slammed his brawny frame onto the dusty ground.

Ford died right there, less than twenty feet from the once-peaceful waters of Webster Springs.

The startled Poole wheeled around, only to see Sarah Crenshaw walking up on Ford's body, triggering more shots into the fallen outlaw as she moved, until Sarah's gun began clicking on spent cartridges.

Still gripped by the fear of Ford's vicious attempt to rape her, Sarah was in no way conscious of her actions.

The marshal walked over and gently removed the gun from her hand, taking the frightened woman firmly into his arms. Their lips melted together, with neither one of them certain who initiated it.

When they parted, Poole could see no pleasure in Sarah's eyes. Nothing could be seen in them but fear and regret. "What's the matter, Sarah? Did I do something wrong?"

"No, you didn't, Braxton, but you and I both know that I did. I suppose you'll have to arrest me now," she said, sticking out her hands so he could slap the cuffs on her two wrists.

Poole was bewildered. "Arrest you? What for?" he said, leading her over to a place next to the campfire. Sam followed along and the three of them sat down.

Sarah couldn't believe his question. "Isn't that why you're here, Braxton? Didn't you and Olsen come to take me in," she replied, fearful of talking in specifics in front of the boy, "for what I did to Ben?"

For a time, Poole was uncertain how to respond. He wanted to laugh, but figured the death of someone, even as bad as Ben Crenshaw, wasn't really a subject for humor. Still, he was amused by Sarah's questions and behavior.

"No, Sarah, you're not under arrest, but I do know all about what happened back at your ranch."

"Then you also know about what I did to Ben?"

Poole nodded. "Yes, Sarah, I do."

"And you're not going to arrest me for . . . for, hurting him, I mean?" asked Sarah, still conscious that Sam's little ears were nearby. "I only did it to protect Sam, after Ben struck him, out of nothing more than anger towards me."

Poole was relieved to finally hear Sarah's clarification of the incident, confirming what he already suspected.

"Miles and I guessed that's what happened," Poole said, going on to enlighten Sarah about the young gambler and the part he played in her husband's death, back in the kitchen of their ranch house. "The wound you inflicted may have been a mortal one, but you ultimately aren't responsible for Ben's passing. A young gambler shot and killed your husband. Kicking Deer later killed him."

The realization of everything Poole explained left the woman shaken and in a state of disbelief. "So, you really aren't here to arrest me."

Poole laughed and took her hand. "I think we've already been over this. No, Sarah, Miles and I came to help you. You're not wanted by the law. As a matter of fact, you and Sam should be able to live pretty comfortably with your portion of the reward money from these three outlaws."

"But I didn't kill them, Braxton; you did."

"Maybe so, but I want half the money to go to you. The rest is to be given to Miles' widow," Poole said, nodding his head towards the body of Bill Ford. "Besides, you're definitely the one who snuffed out his candle. And the world's going to be a better place because of it."

Poole let go of Sarah's hand and stood to his feet. "I need to go take care of Miles," he said, with a look of profound regret. "Then I'll tidy up things here. In the morning, after I retrieve our horses, we'll head back to town. Is that all right with you?"

"That's fine with me." Sarah reached up and placed a tender hand on his shoulder. "In the meantime, can I get you anything?"

Exhausted from his journey, the losses and hardships he faced over the past two days, Poole sat back down and cast a longing glance towards Webster Springs. "Well, there is one thing, Sarah. I'd give just about anything for a cool drink of water."

— The End —

About the Author

R.G. Yoho is a West Virginia native with a passion for history and tales of the American West. Raised on a cattle farm, he is the prolific author of multiple Western novels, along with works of fiction and nonfiction. Yoho is a former president of the West Virginia Writers. Living with his wife near the banks of the Ohio River, Yoho is also a proud member of the Western Writers of America.

Coming Soon!

R.G. YOHO

America's History is His Story

America's History is His Story, is a daily devotional of history and patriotism. If you embrace the power of the Christian faith, if you love the United States of America, if you cherish your family, and if you respect the contributions of our brave military personnel, then you should love this book. Each daily reading is brimming with the qualities of faith, family and freedom.

**For more information
visit:** www.SpeakingVolumes.us

Now Available!

R.G. YOHO'S

ACTION/ADVENTURE WESTERNS

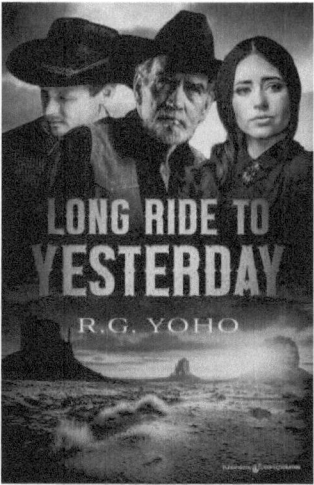

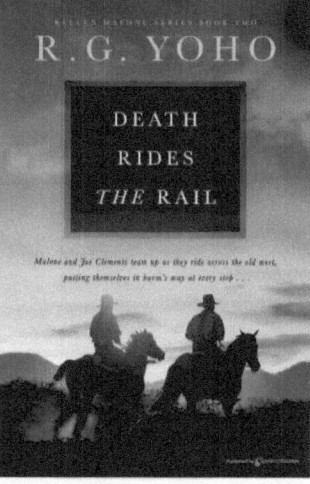

**For more information
visit: www.SpeakingVolumes.us**

Now Available!

ROD MILLER'S

ACTION/ADVENTURE WESTERNS

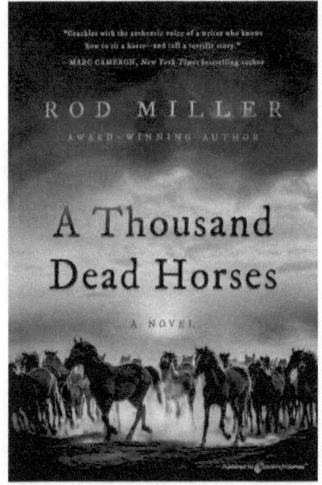

**For more information
visit:** www.SpeakingVolumes.us

www.ingramcontent.com/pod-product-compliance
Lightning Source LLC
LaVergne TN
LVHW041841070526
838199LV00045BA/1380